KU-202-457

TERRY WOGAN

Those Were
the Days

PAN BOOKS

First published 2015 by Macmillan

This paperback edition published 2016 by Pan Books
an imprint of Pan Macmillan
20 New Wharf Road, London N1 9RR
Associated companies throughout the world
www.panmacmillan.com

ISBN 978-1-4472-9826-7

Copyright © Terry Wogan, 2015

The right of Terry Wogan to be identified as the
author of this work has been asserted by him in accordance
with the Copyright, Designs and Patents Act 1988.

All rights reserved. No part of this publication may be reproduced,
stored in a retrieval system, or transmitted, in any form, or by any means
(electronic, mechanical, photocopying, recording or otherwise)
without the prior written permission of the publisher.

Pan Macmillan does not have any control over, or any responsibility for,
any author or third-party websites referred to in or on this book.

3 5 7 9 8 6 4 2

A CIP catalogue record for this book is available from the British Library.

Illustrations by Fred van Deelen

Printed and bound by CPI Group (UK) Ltd, Croydon, CR0 4YY

This book is sold subject to the condition that it shall not, by way of
trade or otherwise, be lent, hired out, or otherwise circulated without
the publisher's prior consent in any form of binding or cover other than
that in which it is published and without a similar condition including
this condition being imposed on the subsequent purchaser.

Visit **www.panmacmillan.com** to read more about all our books
and to buy them. You will also find features, author interviews and
news of any author events, and you can sign up for e-newsletters
so that you're always first to hear about our new releases.

For my wife, family and absent friends

Put it down to impatience, low attention span, or a tendency to make things up as I go along, but I've never been a long-distance writer. These tales are figments of imagination and youthful experience, tied very loosely together by what might have been . . . the fulfilment of a young Irish bank clerk's dream of the ultimate prize: Branch Manager!

Prologue: The Manager

He wondered where the years had gone . . . here he was, back at the same old bank, only this time, as Tom, the manager. No more Tommy, the junior. He'd always hated being called Tommy. And it wasn't the same old bank either. The place had been gutted, refurbished. The forbidding front, the heavy doors had gone, in the interests of 'consumer friendliness'. Instead it was now a glass-fronted building, you could see right in from the street, and the staff at the bank were on show, along with all the new fixtures and fittings. The bank was actually making itself open to its customers. What would his old manager, the imperious and forbidding Charlie, have made of it? Tom thought the refurbishment of the Cattle Market branch with its plush chairs and fancy hangings had been wasted on their regular customers. A trough and some hay would be better suited to them. Ah, the good old days, when customers knew their place, subservient and grateful for any crumb that fell from the manager's table. Bank managers were 'sirs' and – in some of the little country places in which he had made his steady climb from junior, to teller, to cashier, to assistant, to the final glory of 'manager' – they carried the same authority as the local parish priest.

And here he was, after the long and sometimes weary years, his hair starting to get its first flecks of grey. He'd dragged his long-suffering wife Maureen and the two kids all over the country, from deepest Donegal to Dublin and back, to arrive where he started, in the bloody Cattle Market branch. But Maureen had understood. After all, she'd worked for the bank herself before they had the children. It was how they'd met. She'd been by his side ever since the early days and Tom knew he wouldn't have come this far without her. Tom had made manager for the first time in Donegal; nothing much, a little country branch, but pretty good for his age. They were obviously getting him ready for bigger things, and this was it. The Prodigal returned, as manager of the shiny new glass-fronted version of the old place where he started.

They'd called him into Head Office, and sat him at a large table, foostered about, until some old bollocks finally told him that they were going to make him manager of the new branch, as if he were handing him the Holy Grail. He was grateful, but tired. It had been a long haul.

Today was Opening Day. The bank was having a party, and he was the host. Banks never used to have parties, least of all ones to which they invited their customers. It was a mistake, and he was stuck with it, a sacrificial lamb on the altar of modern bank thinking.

The Bank

Tom stood there, looking at the tables full of food and drink, anticipating when the porter would open the new doors: in they'd come, the customers, like ravening wolves, and he knew that nothing would ever be the same again.

How would they ever know their place again, after they'd stood at the same table, drunk the same drink, ate the same sandwiches as their betters? It was different in the old days . . .

Looking back, it was okay, working in the bank. Lots of other guys, who hadn't done well enough in their exams to get into university, or whose parents couldn't afford it, were on the training course. The hours were great: in before half nine, out at half three. As a young man all Tom had to worry about was which branch he was going to be sent to. On the day, a couple of the fellows got the short straw and were sent off to the back of beyond in Donegal. One lucky bugger got Head Office, some other unfortunate, Sligo. They'd be filling out application forms for the Hong Kong and Shanghai before the day was out, but Tom's luck held. He got a Dublin branch – not the cream of the crop, and a manager who was supposed to be a bit of a martinet, but it was close enough to go home for lunch. The bank closed for lunch from 1 p.m. to 2 p.m. and opened again until 3 p.m. It wasn't there for the convenience of the customers. When you met the customers, it didn't seem such a bad idea to keep them at a distance . . .

*

The little man came in, once a week, on market day. The bank was known as the 'Cattle Market' branch, so the little chap had every right to make a hard-earned lodgement of cash to his account, having toiled amid the mud, the droppings, the noisome stench of a thousand head of cattle, all morning. The trouble was, he carried his work with him, on his boots, his clothes, his cap, his very pores. And his bank-notes. Long after he'd left the bank, to begin herding the cattle through the streets of Dublin to the Docks, for shipment to foreign lands eager for Irish beef, the scent of the cow-byre lingered, and

mingled with that of the fish and chip shop propri-
etor, a friendly Italian from across the road, whose
hat and clothes were redolent of all that was worst
in fried coley and ancient fat. The manager of the
pub next door brought something with him as well,
a heavy breath of the brewery, with particular refer-
ence to the beneficial aromas of Arthur Guinness.
Then the farmers would traipse in, having come into
town from the outback a couple of miles away, in
cars with ten years of dirt on them, and a small cow
or a couple of pigs in the back seat. There was no
use, they said, putting the animals in the boot; the
lock was broken, and it was pointless to try to tie
them down with hairy twine. Some were miserable,
constantly complaining about their lot, and the price
they were being offered for their chickens, always
leading to the mutterings of underpaid bank clerks
along the lines of, 'You never see a farmer on a bike'.
Other sons of the soil were full of hearty banter and
rural bonhomie, hoping to bluff the bank manager
into an injudicious loan. No chance. He was a banker
of the old school, who believed banks were for taking
money in, not giving it out. It wouldn't have mattered
if you were related to the Archbishop, you wouldn't
get a loan or overdraft of more than 10 per cent of

your total assets. Under the mattress, that was the only place for your money. All the customers bore bravely the unmistakeable whiff of their daily toil in the fields and farmyards. Five lousy quid a week seemed poor enough recompense to a bank clerk who had to have himself and his clothes fumigated every week at his own expense, with no chance of the kindly bank manager offering him so much as a nose-peg, let alone a gas-mask.

Around twelve every day, a different scent wafted down to join the inhalatory mayhem from the little kitchen upstairs, where the porter was preparing the manager's lunch. It was not part of the porter's duties, whose job description included opening and closing the bank, sweeping the floor, and accompanying the junior clerk as he carried old bank-notes, many still smelling of the Cattle Market, to be exchanged at Head Office for crisp new ones, and then returning on public transport with splendid disregard for every casual thief, mugger and thug. On his return, the porter made his way to the local grocer where he purchased the manager's lunch. He would have been better off with a bank standing order, because the manager ate the same lunch every day: lamb chop, potatoes and peas. What the manager never knew was that the porter, something of a socialist rebel, was deeply resentful of being expected to cook lunch, even for the manager. Occasionally, if you listened from the foot of the stairs, a low thumping could be heard from the direction of the bank's kitchen. This was the sound of the manager's chop being tenderized, by the simple expedient of being kicked around the little room by the porter, before being popped in the pan. So, from twelve onwards, the smell of a frying lamb chop and the more subtle savours of boiled peas and potatoes added to the heady nasal congestion of the Cattle Market branch.

It was said that the sailors who manned the submarines of the Second World War got so used to the permanent fug and oppressive atmosphere of the restricted space on board, underwater for days on end, that when the submarine surfaced and the sailors got the chance to breathe fresh air, they threw up. It was also said by Tom and the other clerks of the Cattle Market branch that they only left the bank at the end of business slowly, with careful steps, to avoid a sudden attack of biliousness if they took a gulp of fresh air too quickly.

Rather like deep-sea divers heedful of the dreaded

'bends', the wary clerks staggered first to the internal door, shutting it behind them, waited for five minutes for their breathing to adjust to near normality, before opening the front door, bit by bit, breathing in, breathing out, and then, a deep breath, and bravely forward into fresh air – hoping that the wind from the market was blowing the other way . . .

Sheila's Tale

People don't think much of bankers these days, but the bank had been good for Tom. He'd met Maureen in the bank, they'd been happy together. She'd stuck with him through the years of moving from branch to branch without complaint at being uprooted time and time again; they had a reasonable social life wherever his rising star had landed them. The pair of them rubbed along quite nicely together and all in all their marriage had been a happy one. Although sometimes Tom wondered if she was yearning for a different life. He thought back to Sheila – now there was someone he often thought about – was she truly happy with Sean as he was with Maureen?

Sheila had been Tom's childhood sweetheart. Their schools were near each other, and for a time it looked as though Sheila and Tom might go straight from the classroom to the church together, like so many of their friends had done. But Sheila had been a real live-wire and clever too; she was ambitious and longed for adventure. Tom didn't hold her attention for long. But over the years their paths had crossed, news travelled fast in small towns, and Tom had been amused to find that Sheila became a banker's wife after all . . .

*

Sheila was past fifty before she realized, once and for all, that it was never going to happen. None of it. She was never going to ride on the back of a Vespa through the streets of Rome with anybody who looked like Gregory Peck; never going to be rich, or famous. Never meet the Pope, curtsey to the Queen, or watch the tennis at Wimbledon from the Royal Box. Never walk the red carpet at a movie premiere, or sit in the front row at a Paris fashion show.

She'd been popular at school, a leader, but never captain. Good at games, just not quite good enough to make the school team at tennis. Clever, but not enough to win anything at the school's prize-giving. The nuns could find no fault with her; she worked hard to win their approval, and she won a medal for her attention to her religious studies. Even then, she had a suspicion that it was never quite enough, she wanted more. She felt destined for more, even for greatness. She knew she was pretty, everybody told her so. They told her that she could be a film star, a supermodel. She moved from childhood, through adolescence to young adulthood, but stardom never beckoned . . .

From girls' toys to boys, through teenage romances, dances, the first drink, the first choked cigarette. It was fun, laughing with her friends at the foolishness of boys, how she loved to flirt, making the shy boys blush, leading them on with fluttering eyes and even kisses before firmly slapping them down when they began to paw and grope. They called her a tease, and she loved it, and the power it gave her.

Sheila passed her exams, and thought about university, but she didn't want to spend another three years over books in dreary halls. She wanted to get out into the real world and make her mark. She sent her photos off to a model agency but got no reply, and then someone told her that if she wanted to be an actress she'd have to go to London and join an acting school. Mummy and Daddy would never allow that, their precious daughter all alone in a city of sin. Anyway, she'd worry about that later, for now there was Jim, who she'd met at the tennis-club hop, the first fellow she'd really been attracted to. He had a bit of a reputation among the crowd for being a ladies' man, and it excited her that he'd chosen her, so she'd let him go a little bit further than the other boys. After a couple of months, he left. Off to England to a summer job in a packing factory, to make a few quid before settling down to work in his old man's hardware store. He promised to write, but he never did, and she had a feeling in the pit of her stomach that he'd never come back. A few years later, she heard on the grapevine that he'd married an English girl, and was very happy with two lovely children and running a pub in Liverpool.

Sheila went on a girls' trip to Sitges, in Spain, to get over Jim, and flung herself with as close to abandon as she could into sunshine-filled days on the beach and sangria-fuelled nights in the clubs. She swam and danced and drank the days and nights away, flirting and kissing and letting herself go further with a waiter than she'd ever allowed Jim.

She came back with a tan, and a taste for Bacardi and Coke, but after a few days the euphoria passed, and nothing had changed. Her father suggested she sit for the bank exams; she passed, and was offered a post as a secretary in the bank's head office. It meant moving to Dublin, and she felt that she was at last getting somewhere. Her mother wasn't all that keen – those city lads couldn't be trusted. Luckily, her mother's sister lived in Dublin, and could put her up, and keep an eye on her.

The first month she was lonely, intimidated by the formality of the bank, stifled by her aunt's strict restrictions on her coming and going, and missing her friends. It was inevitable that she'd fall for the first person that took any notice of her. One of her fellow secretaries encouraged her to go to a dance staged by the bank's social club, and there he was, Sean. He was tall, not bad-looking, a terrible dancer, but with a nice smile, and an easy manner. He was a cashier at Head Office, pretty good for a fellow in his mid-thirties, with every chance of a managership before he was forty. He took her out for a pint at a pub in Ballsbridge and dropped her back to her aunt's in his Morris Minor, without even pressing for a kiss. Her aunt was impressed. As the relationship developed he took her out to a little Greek restaurant called the Trocadero. Sheila had never had moussaka before; she loved it, it was foreign, exciting. It didn't happen all the time, she knew that Sean wasn't made of money, and they often just went back to Sean's house, where his parents made her very welcome, after they all recited the family Rosary.

It was inevitable. A whirlwind romance, by Ireland's standards, saw them engaged within a year, and a year later they were married. They went to Torremolinos on their honeymoon; it wasn't as exciting as her memories of Sitges and the girlie holiday, but Sean was not too demanding of his marital rights, and gentle. They came back to a little rented flat on the Southside of the city, and went to work at Head Office together on the bus. They ate together in the staff canteen, and returned home on the same bus. They went out to the movies once a week, and very occasionally to the Trocadero for old times' sake; the waiters were always glad to see them.

Sean's banking talents took them all over the country, from the Midlands to the West, to the final accolade of a managership in Donegal. Along the way, there were two children, both university graduates, and now living in Dublin.

In Letterkenny, County Donegal, she was the respected wife of the bank manager, a popular member of the golf club, a regular at the bridge club, and wondering what had happened to all those dreams of her youth. But Sean would be home in an hour, wanting his tea.

Making for the Exit

The porter opened the new glass doors, and in they came, like savages who'd never had a bite to eat or a drop to drink in their lives. Tom had watched them mooching about for ages in the street, the pub manager, the chippie owner who cooked the oldest fish and the worst chips in town without ever taking his hat off, the florid farmers, the cattle jobbers, the old geezers glad of something to do. And the chancers who'd never had a bank account in their lives, sneaking in on the expectation of something for nothing. The old manager, now retired, was cheery conviviality itself to all and sundry, welcoming his old customers with a warmth he rarely displayed when he held their accounts in a vice. The martinet had become Charlie Charm, apart from persisting in calling him Tommy, the old git. Retirement certainly suited 'Charlie', everybody agreed, but as for the real Michael, well that was another story . . .

*

Michael had been looking forward to it since he turned sixty. Early retirement, with a decent pension based on his last year's salary, topped up by the old age pension. They had no mortgage, he'd managed to put a bit away in the bank after the kids had left, and it was going to be downhill all the way until he popped his clogs. With any luck on the health front, the wife and himself would have a comfortable twenty years to go from the day his employer presented him with the goodbye clock.

Most evenings, after what he and herself still called 'tea', he would enthuse about the times they would have together, and all the time in the world to enjoy them. He avidly read the travel sections of the Sunday newspapers, those wonderful cruises and escorted tours, imagining the marvellous experiences they would share.

Now, a year into his anticipated days of freedom from the monotony of the daily grind, a leisurely life of time together and the pursuit of pleasures denied them in the past, he had to admit to himself, if to nobody else, and certainly not to his wife, that it hadn't quite worked out as planned.

The accolades from the boss, the fond farewells of workmates, even the presentation of the bloody clock had, he felt, been a genuine tribute to his almost life-long contribution to the firm. He was never going to make it to the very top, but he'd been popular enough when younger, and respected as a wise old head as the years slipped inexorably by.

The big day came and went, the first day of the rest of his and his wife's life stretched ahead, bright with promise . . .

It came as a surprise, as early as the first week of the idyll, when he found himself alone in the house, with only the dog for company, for much of the day. For his wife had a busy social life, developed over the years. Ladies' golf day at the club took up most of Tuesday morning, with lunch taking the ladies well into the afternoon. On Wednesday, the day was given over to bridge and tea at one or the other of his wife's friends' houses; Thursday was the day when the ladies lunched at a local gastro-pub, and Friday was shopping day.

He decided, although he hated shopping, to join his wife on the expedition to the supermarket. 'Or I'll never see you at all,' as he put it, with more than a hint of pathos.

It was to be the one and only time they walked the supermarket aisles together.

When they got home, she sat him down with a cup of tea, and some home truths:

'Michael,' she said, 'for the past thirty years, while you've been out to work, I've been running this house, paying the bills, watching the pennies, making sure there's always something on the table. I don't need you checking every receipt, and I certainly don't want you following me around the supermarket like you did this morning, with your endless questions about everything I was buying, and picking things off the shelves and putting them in the basket, for me to put back on the shelf, because we'd never use them. And chatting to the checkout girl as if she were an old friend, while everybody in the queue behind was getting more and more annoyed with the delay. With all your foostering around, it took an hour longer than usual, and you ended up making me late for my book club meeting. Never again. Find yourself something to do on a Friday; you're sitting around the house moping far too much since you retired, and I haven't got all day to sit and talk to you.'

But he had no one else to talk to. His next door neighbour was still working, and, apart from the odd remark about the weather, he had never spoken to the other retiree, down the road.

He'd left all his acquaintances and friends behind at work. All his socializing had been done with them: the firm's annual dinner, the corporate weekends, the charity golf days. Any local friends were those his wife had made for him, the couples with whom they shared the occasional dinner or drinks party, but he'd never had the time or inclination to strike up any kind of closer friendship with the husbands, and it was a little late in the day for chatting up their wives.

He'd let his membership of the golf club go, because he had felt too tired after a hard week's work to get up at all hours on a Saturday morning to be on the first tee. He knew better than to suggest a round of golf with his wife. In their earlier, more enthusiastic sporting days, they had tried to play together, but they always ended up not speaking after a couple of holes. He knew that it was his fault, but he couldn't stop himself telling her what was wrong with her game . . . He never really understood why anybody would take such offence at a piece of well-meaning advice. All right, he was no Jack Nicklaus himself, but there was never any need for walking off the course in a huff.

He still pored over the travel brochures looking at the cruises to all the places he'd never been, but he knew in his heart of hearts that they would always be just dreams. Every time he tentatively mentioned the possibility of an exotic trip to get away from the boredom that surrounded him, his wife would knock it on the head. Her social round had few windows of opportunity, and even if she could have found the time, there were birthdays, anniversaries, all manner of commitments that could not be avoided.

She knew well enough his disappointment with the failure of what had been his dream of freedom, but it had come as no surprise to her, for she had been dreading his retirement more and more as the years went by. She knew that he would be under her feet and lifting his feet for the vacuum cleaner, getting in the way in the kitchen, and all the other irritants that friends whose husbands had retired had warned her about.

He became a regular viewer of daytime TV. He'd make himself a sandwich, settle back and really enjoy it, and get very irritated by any interruptions of the phone or doorbell to *Countdown* or *The Chase*. His wife was usually in by five, but they stuck to the old routine of never having a drink until after half six, a glass or two of wine with dinner, TV, and off up to bed at ten thirty.

Making for the Exit

People occasionally asked him how retirement was suiting him, and he always said he felt so well, he didn't know why he hadn't done it years earlier.

The Happy Couple

Tom wasn't surprised to see the couple with the joint account arrive first through the doors; the husband always looked like he'd be early for his own funeral. Liam and Nuala Houlihan he knew well: he'd been at school with Liam, they'd packed down in the same school rugby team, and kept in touch, although Liam had gone on to university, while Tom toiled behind a desk in the service of the bank. Tom and Maureen had been to their wedding, and a year later, the Houlihans had been to theirs. They asked each other to dinner, and there was a bit of a competition between Maureen and Nuala over the cooking, which was all right by Liam and himself, they'd both spent too many years with the overcooked vegetables and rice puddings of their beloved mothers. Tom thanked God that the country was finally emerging from the trough of despond that had been Irish cooking for centuries.

Liam and Nuala always seemed very happy, but

Tom had noticed recently a little niggle here and there.

He mentioned it to Maureen, who'd seen it as well, even earlier. 'It's Liam,' she said, 'he'd get on anybody's nerves.'

Tom couldn't believe it, he'd never noticed anything. 'Liam's a decent fellow, bit of a worrier, but he's a teacher, that's enough to make anyone twitchy.'

'He's always rushing her everywhere, that's enough to drive anyone mad,' Maureen said.

'Yes,' said Tom, 'but he rushed her off her feet into marriage, and she didn't complain then. I hope she won't forget that.'

*

It got on Nuala's nerves, his obsession with being on time. Whenever they went anywhere together, when he'd finished nagging her as she sat in front of the dressing table, he'd be downstairs, shouting at her that he didn't know what was keeping her, he'd had his coat on and been ready to go for half an hour, and it wouldn't be worth going at all, they were going to be so late. By the time she made her way slowly downstairs, he'd be fussing about, holding her coat, the front door open, the car started. Of course, Liam hadn't checked whether all the windows were closed, or the kitchen door locked, so while he fumed, she carefully checked everything, including the gas hobs, which, she reminded him, he'd left on once before, and it was a miracle that the whole house hadn't gone up in flames.

In the car, on the way to the party, he complained bitterly, as he always did, about having to go out in the middle of the week when he had to get up for work early next morning, and he'd never liked any of the crowd that were going to this party, could she not have said that they were busy, and couldn't come? She didn't reply; she'd heard it all before, and she couldn't be bothered having a row, with the pair of them arriving at the Murphys' not talking to each other, with faces like thunder. And she knew all too well that Mairead Murphy would spot their domestic upheaval like lightning, and pretend to sympathize on the phone next morning. She also knew that her husband would be chatting away and flirting with anything in a skirt as soon as he got a couple of drinks inside him, despite his balding head and growing paunch.

The gracious hostess Mairead greeted them with smiles and kisses, shouting up the stairs, 'Cormac!

It's the Houlihans! Are you out of the bath? Get down here, you eejit, and start pouring the drinks! Thank God I got ready early myself, or you'd have been knocking on the door for ages. You're the first to arrive.'

Nuala didn't even bother giving her husband her death look, she'd got so used to the surprise that always greeted them on their arrival anywhere. Liam, oblivious as ever, remarked favourably on the wallpaper, the curtains and the carpet in the living room, as the host rushed in, his hair still wet, in bare feet and dressing gown. 'I lose all track of time in the bath,' he laughed. 'I can't believe it's eight o'clock. I was sure we asked you for half-past. Still, you're here now, what'll it be for booze?'

She thought: Much more of this, and I'll leave him . . .

Cormac poured the drinks, a couple of hefty vodka and tonics, 'Ice and lemon?', and they were on their own, while he went back upstairs to get dressed and Mairead could be heard pot-walloping in the kitchen. 'Well,' she said, 'here we are again, on our own, in someone's lounge, the hosts thinking we're mad to have arrived so early, and no one else in sight.'

The Happy Couple

'Manners,' he said mildly. 'My mother always said it's good manners and courtesy to the hosts to arrive on time, the mark of a gentleman.'

Her iron self-control finally abandoned, she snarled, 'Your mother and her good manners! It's the mark of a social cripple to arrive anywhere hours before anyone else!' After that, there was nothing to be said. She stood by the window, he by the fireplace. It was ten minutes before she saw the lights of the car of the next guests, and a good half hour before all had arrived. It was another hour before everyone had downed a couple of Cormac's stiff drinks and Mairead was able to chivvy them all into the dining room.

She found herself sitting between Chris and Bart, neither of whom showed the slightest interest in her or her life. When she could get a word in, she asked them about their families, but they talked only about themselves, and to each other, across her. Bart's talk was of his son, potentially an Irish rugby fly-half of the future, and his daughter, whose difficult choice was between being an actress or a supermodel like her mother. Chris's monologue was about how he had flourished on his own in the advertising world, since telling the boss at his last place where to get off.

He was stuck between Orla and Eileen, and in pursuance of his lone social furrow of good manners, solicited their views on everything from feminism to their families. They never asked him about his views, or himself. Orla had just turned down a chance to sing at a big musical event in Croke Park because she felt she couldn't give the time, her children came first. Eileen couldn't have agreed more, although her children were never a trouble; Colin, her son, was a little bit wild, but, sure, weren't all boys of his age. His father was a bit of a boy when a young fellow too.

Afterwards, everybody went back to the lounge and Orla was persuaded to sing, after many modest refusals; then, with many a promise of lunches, dinners and meetings, and fulsome thanks to the hosts, the guests dispersed to their cars.

They had been at opposite ends of the table, and hadn't spoken since her bitter words earlier, before the others arrived. As they drove home, it was she who broke the silence: 'Ice and lemon? What else would you have in your vodka and tonic, a half of Guinness? That meat was like leather – what was it?'

'I think it started out as lamb, but finished up as charcoal. Burnt to a cinder.'

The Happy Couple

'Do you wonder?' Nuala said. 'We didn't sit down to eat until half nine. And the conversation! Bart going on about his thick son, whose brains are all in his feet, and Chris pretending that he hadn't got the sack.'

'Don't be talking,' Liam said. 'Eileen making out that her toe-rag of a son, doing community service for beating up another young fella, was just a "little bit wild, like his father", who was a drunken thug when I first met him. And poor Orla, still thinking she can sing. Croke Park, my eye, she'd empty the place in five minutes.'

'That singing was pathetic,' she agreed. 'Why do they keep making her do it?' She paused. 'Ice and lemon! A supermodel, like her mother!' They both choked with the laughter.

As they went through their front door, she kissed him. 'Let's go straight to bed,' she said.

Never Say Goodbye

Tom smiled to himself as he thought of another couple, the O'Hallorans. They'd taken a mortgage at the bank years ago and had been loyal customers ever since. They'd be along in a minute, not too early like the Houlihans, but he knew which pair would be the last to leave.

James and Sinead O'Halloran were a slightly older couple, living on the Northside of town not far from himself and Maureen. They met occasionally at mutual acquaintances' parties, and their kids went to the same schools, although the O'Hallorans' kids were a few years older. Outside of the bank, when James would occasionally come in to cash a cheque, the other place the couples would meet was the school, at prize days or parent-teacher meetings. Tom remembered his own schooldays. No such thing as parent-teacher meetings then. Parents knew their place, which was well down in the pecking order behind Christian Brothers and Jesuits, as far as education was concerned. They had no say in the matter of the teaching of their children, indeed to query it would be regarded as nothing short of an impertinence. The very idea, thinking that a parent might know better than the Church about a child's upbringing.

The Christian Brothers were pretty free with their fists, and ruled the classroom by fear and what could only be described as brutality, if their pupils' descriptions were anything to go by. Tom used to thank his lucky stars that his parents scraped up enough money to send him to the Jesuit school, where the brutality was at least controlled. They didn't hit you a box on the ear for nothing, just took your hands off with a leather if your homework wasn't up to scratch.

The big sin of his childhood was pride. Sex was neither discussed nor encouraged, and 'only in its infancy in Ireland', as the wiseacres used to say. But 'showing off', boasting, displaying anything other than a becoming modesty, was regarded as an indication that an individual has 'lost the run of themselves'. Tom wondered how anyone who grew up in Ireland could ever have any self-esteem whatsoever. Yet the country was up to its armpits in people who couldn't stop talking.

Not a lot of shyness about that he could see, and particularly all around him at the bank's party. It was like the Tower of Babel. He joined James and Sinead O'Halloran as they arrived, for a bit of peace and quiet. She was a cheerful creature, but James took a bit of getting to know, and having met him at parties, he certainly gave you plenty of time to know him.

*

Whether it was a funeral, wedding, christening, dinner, lunch, or a meeting in the office, James was always the last to leave. He'd love to have been able to say goodbye, or cheers! or ciao! like all the rest who were long gone, but he was incapable of making an exit. He wanted to be the only person left in the room, the last man standing. Then, there would be nobody left to talk about him behind his back.

At meetings, when he finally, reluctantly, made to leave, he was all too conscious of the relief on other faces, and, as he shut the door behind him, he strained to hear what was said. He never heard anybody say, 'Jaysus, I thought he'd never go', but he always knew it was on their minds. People who didn't know him felt that he showed great respect to the deceased, standing over the grave long after the other mourners had gone, but he didn't want any acid comments made by his leaving the burial early. At dinner parties, he always stood up as others prepared to leave, but sat down again when it was clear that not everyone was on their way. When it became apparent that there was only him, his wife and the hosts left at the table, he would make his way to the door, but never open it until he could think of something funny to say. Usually, his wife would push past him as he struggled for the bon mot, and then, they'd be out in the hallway, where he would delay putting on his overcoat and try to start a new conversation with his exhausted hostess, before his wife finally forced him through the door.

Most of the time he had no idea why he was doing it, or that he was postponing the fond farewell at all, but every so often his wife, who liked a bit of a chat herself, would say under her breath, 'James! For God's sake, people will think we have no home to go to!' Then it would occur to him that he might have outstayed his welcome. He ignored the thought.

He enjoyed people, he liked their company; what was the harm?

He got engaged to Sinead after a long courtship, precipitated by her blunt-spoken father, who took

him aside after a Sunday tea, which his lack of move-
ment to go home had prolonged to the late evening,
and said: 'And when will you be giving her the ring?'
There was nothing to be said after that, although he
wasn't sure whether he was in love with Sinead, but
he didn't want her relations complaining that he was
stringing her along, and her girlfriends bad-mouthing
him if he broke it off. He didn't know how to get out
of it without everybody thinking he was a loser, so
they went around to the Ring King together, and it
was all done and dusted. Everybody said that they
were delighted, of course, his friends slapping him on
the back: 'Ah, the hard man! You're a lucky devil!'
But he was sure that behind his back it was: 'What
does she see in him?' 'He must have talked her into
it', 'Poor girl, she'll never have a moment to herself.'

He supposed he was happy, and Sinead certainly
was, a new-found confidence brightening her person-
ality, but he wasn't sure. He thought she was lovely,
but did anybody else? None of the other fellows had
ever said that they wouldn't mind getting 'a leg over
her', which is the way they carried on over girls they
fancied, but maybe they said it behind his back. And
what did she see in him anyway? Hadn't he heard his
father and mother discussing him, years ago, when

he was still at school? 'Well, what are we going to do with James? He's not much good at anything, is he?'

'Ah now,' he heard his mother say, 'sure, he may not be the brightest, and he could do with being a bit taller, but he's got a good heart.'

His parents were kind, but as he grew older, he felt that they were tolerating him, encouraging him to go out and get a job, rather than go to university, – an opinion shared by his teachers, one of whom he heard say, 'Ah, yer man hasn't a bad bone in his body, but he'd be better off learning a trade.'

So as soon as he finished at school, he got a job in insurance, his father having a bit of pull in the right quarters. It was all right, enough money to run an old Morris Minor, a pint with the boys at the pub on a Saturday, the tennis-club hop on a Sunday. He wasn't very good with girls; he once caught one of them laughing at him behind his back, or so he thought, but he met Sinead there, and she seemed to like him, although for a long time he couldn't be sure, and he'd go into a furious jealous sulk for hours if she even looked at anyone else.

She was calm and gentle, and every so often he caught her giving him a look that he didn't really understand.

Never Say Goodbye

The wedding was lovely, so everybody said, but he wasn't sure. They laughed at his speech, and cheered, but as he sat down, he thought he'd heard a jeer. The best man got the biggest laugh of the day when he said that James would be leaving first, for the only time in his life . . .

A happy marriage to a wife who understood, and who he didn't have to keep in conversation, and a couple of children with the attention span of butterflies calmed his need for reassurance that nobody, at home at least, was whispering behind his back. He still found it difficult to get through the office door without leaving on a laugh, and a moment listening for the reaction, but at social occasions that old look from his wife allayed his fears.

It had taken him too long to understand that look. Now, he knew. It was love. And if the most important person in his world never laughed behind his back, he knew he could safely shut up in front of others.

The Eternal Optimist

After only a couple of drinks, the noise level was louder than ever acceptable in any respectable bank, and the smile of welcome on Tom's face was beginning to feel like a rictus of death. And that old boy, Paddy, who kept asking loudly if the red or white wine was the only drink available, and whether a pint of stout was out of the question for one of 'the bank's oldest and best customers', reminded Tom of his late father-in-law. What a character he'd been; he'd never lost that child-like belief that the world revolved around him. Tom remembered sitting with him watching television, when one of Padraig's sons burst into the room, returning home for the first time after twenty years in Australia. He'd flown around the world, taken the train, then a taxi, returning from the Lucky Country to the Old One for probably his last meeting with the old folks at home. The long weary journey was wasted on Padraig; Australia might as well be just around the corner, as far as he was concerned. The world started and ended with him. Continuing to watch the television, he didn't rise from his chair, or even turn around to greet a long-lost son. 'Howya,' Padraig said.

Born and bred in Galway, on the hungry west coast of Ireland, where, centuries before, the hated Cromwell had sent the native Irish over the Shannon river to 'Hell or Connaught' to make room on the richer pastures for English settlers, Padraig left as soon as he could for the bright lights of Dublin. Tall for an Irishman of his time, and particularly one from the poor West, with a head of auburn hair and a forceful, confident manner that masked the insecurity he carried throughout his life, he blustered his way into a job as a 'grocer's curate', living above the shop and paid a pittance to do all the heavy work, like tying up and lifting the bags of sugar and cereals. It was a long time before the boss let him near the counter to serve the customers, but when he did, they warmed to his hearty country manner. After a time, he was even allowed to use the bacon slicer, a dangerous contraption with a razor-like circular blade rotated to slice the customers' bacon and ham to their liking.

Long before the rigours of Health and Safety that

keep us all from death and destruction these days, bacon slicers then did not have a safety guard. Engaging in rough banter with the lady customer as he finely sliced her half-pound of cooked ham, Padraig took his eye off the blade, and damn nearly severed his thumb. They took him to hospital, where they staunched the flow of blood, and stitched his hand up. They didn't do a great job, but he was back at work the following day, heavily bandaged, pale but determined, and with a hand that he was never able to use properly again.

It was a hand he used to his advantage in later life, having moved from Dublin in retirement to a quieter, more rural part of the country where nobody knew him, and he could fantasize in the snug of the local pub to anybody who'd listen – and there were quite a few who wouldn't turn down a free pint, even if it meant having to listen to the old boy's stories.

A gullible young reporter from a local paper was among them, and in a short time the headline read: 'An old IRA man looks back'. It told the brave tale of how Padraig, fighting for Ireland's freedom, exchanging fire with the pursuing Black and Tans, was shot in the hand, and almost bled to death while on the run. The reporter described Padraig's wounded hand sympathetically, evidence of his fight for Ireland's freedom.

Carried away by the role he now firmly believed he had played in the struggle, Padraig moved on to further extravagances. The high command of the IRA had sent him, one of their most reliable gunmen, on a mission to Chicago to put a stop to the Mafia's interference in the running of their fund-raising activities. Padraig recounted the tale of sitting at a table at Johnny Torrio's place in the Windy City. They were all there, Capone, Bugsy and, sitting opposite from him at the table, Legs Diamond. The mood was dangerous, and Padraig quickly recognized that Legs was the man to watch. 'Diamond's hands were moving under the table, but I had him covered with my gat. I'd beaten him to the draw, and he knew it. The Mafia promised to stay away from our fund-raisers.' Padraig's use of the word 'gat' showed him to be an avid reader of gangster novels, but in truth he'd never been outside Ireland in his life. Still, in his stories he was the only man to outdraw Legs Diamond, who, if you remember *The Untouchables*, gunned down Sean Connery.

In his real life, though, Padraig was no eejit. Despite nearly cutting the hand off himself, while handing all manner of vegetables and other comestibles over the counter of the grocery store, he had identified a long-felt need. What the country and its grocers wanted was pre-packed beans, peas, cereals and all the other fiddly nuts and bolts that made a grocer's life a living hell. Ignoring planning restrictions against commercial building in residential areas, Padraig built a small factory in his back garden, and the packaging started. It took off; it expanded, and became too big for any council gobdaw to do anything about. Padraig, who had given up the drink to settle down and have a family, began to enjoy the fruits of his entrepreneurial insight. Of course, Maureen was born late to her father. He was well into his fifties by the time she came along. By then, he was holding court in the lounge of the local golf club, where he bought many a round of drinks and began to spin his Black and Tan yarns. The boy from the West had arrived, and he was going to enjoy it.

Padraig ended his days in a nursing home, but he retained a child-like indifference to the Grim Reaper all his life. When he was eighty, he planted small apple trees in his back garden, fully expecting to reap the benefit. Which he did, ten years later . . .

Those Were the Days

Padraig was a man who lived life as if there were no one else around. He never ate cold meat, nor the skin of a roast chicken, and he liked his soup cooled on the window-ledge of the kitchen at lunchtime. When the family went on a picnic, he was never a man for the cold corned-beef or ham sandwich. Padraig would insist on a starter of hot soup, followed by what he cheerily referred to as 'pig's arse and cabbage' with boiled potatoes in their jackets and a rice pudding. All cooked to perfection on a Primus stove, or he'd want to know why. He retained to the last his conviction that the world revolved around him and no one was going to dissuade him, leaving us, without a bother on him, at 103 . . .

The Da

As Tom surveyed the party in full flow around him, he noticed an old boy, thin strands of hair drawn strategically over his head, just as his Da used to do.

Padraig and Tom's father had what could only be described as an uneasy relationship. The one extrovert, attention-seeking, the other shy, earnest. His wedding being an Irish one, everyone seized the opportunity to speak. Not just to others at their table, or at the bar, greeting total strangers as if they were long-lost friends, secure in the knowledge that they would never have to entertain them, nor even talk to them again, but exercising an Irishman's right to stagger to his feet the worse for drink, and address the room at large. He'd only seen worse at his great friend Jamie's wedding, to a lovely Swedish girl, just outside Malmö, where they seemed to be pulling in passing pedestrians and cyclists to say a few well-chosen words and down a schnapps and a couple of herrings before going on their way. Padraig having spoken fully in his praise of the bride, his own wife, his early life, his family and particularly himself, had sat down to loud applause. Only to rise again, in the middle of Tom's own father's speech, with a few bon mots that he had forgotten to regale the crowd with. The Da wasn't too pleased.

*

Sunday was the Da's only day off. Not that he was allowed to sleep in. The Ma had him up for Mass at eight, in the parish church, and back for rashers and eggs at nine. It wasn't that she was particularly devout, any more than the Da was, but they were respectable people, and there were the neighbours to think about. It was a new church, built for the greater glory of God and the Bishop, and an ideal billet for the new parish priest, a wavy-haired glamour boy who had a way with the ladies. Not that the town needed another Catholic church since there was one on every corner; Franciscan, Redemptorist, Dominican, Jesuit. Still, the new one was handy enough to walk to, and yer man the priest, Father Flanagan, didn't hang around with unnecessary ceremonial or the usual preaching of hell-fire and damnation if you didn't say your prayers, as he had rashers and eggs to go to as well, his housekeeper being no slouch with a pan and skillet.

Sustained by breakfast, the Da would head off on his trusty bike for a bit of fishing, the rod over his shoulder, the tackle firmly attached over the back wheel, a bag with a flask of tea and corned-beef sandwiches on the handlebars. He still stopped at his shop of course, to check that everything was as he'd left it, on Saturday evening. Then on to the river, in the hope that the fish were rising. Not that he cared that much, it was the getting-away, the peace broken only by the songs of the corncrake and skylark, the graceful art of fly-fishing.

It used to take him a good hour before he started fishing: what he really liked was the delicate tying of the flies to his line. He rarely caught a trout, but plenty of eels, which he threw back, knowing well that his wife wouldn't touch them with a barge-pole, never mind cook them. Who ate eels, anyway? Corned-beef sandwiches, now you're talking. On the way home, the Da always stopped for a half-pint of stout at a little pub run by a character called 'Bokkles' Gleeson. It was the way the man pro-nounced 'bottles', and it would probably have gone unremarked if he hadn't been a publican.

Those Were the Days

The Da was in the grocery business; there weren't many careers available to a young man who had fallen out with his old man, and run away from home. So he ended up in a local victuallers, and over the years, with his hard work, attention to detail, meticulous handwriting and perfectly kept finger-nails, he got a job with bigger and better purveyors of foodstuffs to the public, before eventually he was rewarded with the managership of his very own store.

The rise in status, not to mention in his pay packet, enabled him to throw caution to the wind, and marry the Ma.

Every Wednesday evening he'd be up on the bike again, and off to what he called 'the Dogs', grey-hound racing. He never made any money on it, but then, if you're betting in shillings, you can't expect to come back with your pockets stuffed with pound notes. Like every other man of his background, he followed the horses as well, and was a great student of form, although the closest he ever got to a race-course was the bookies. He wasn't without connections in the racing game, for the horse people, the hunting crowd that graced the surrounding green fields and lorded it over the local peasantry, were customers of his grocery store. Who else could sate their desires for foie gras, lychees, stem ginger and dried fish from India? The lords of the manor, the relics of old decency, the remittance men paid to stay away from their families, the trainers, the knackers, the jobbers, the chancers, all beat a path to his little grocery door. None of them ever gave him a tip worth putting a bob on.

The Da treated them as he found them, not being a great man for hierarchies, clerical or otherwise. He hailed from a village that had a virtual caste system: at the top, the lord of the manor, to whom all made obeisance, who never paid his bills – the local trades-men expected to be satisfied with the lord's patronage alone. Next on the totem pole, the lord's factotum, or bailiff, a man to be feared since most of the land on which the villagers lived was managed by him. Then the parish priest, followed by the sergeant of the local police, the doctor and the bank manager. The Da never forgot having to get off the pavement to let any of them pass. Although his relatives continued to live there, he never went back to that village.

He was a singer, a baritone, who when young competed at song contests, but he kept his singing to himself as he grew older. He never sang at Christmas, nor parties. He sang in the bathroom when he shaved, at night before he went to bed. The bathroom was a perfect acoustic setting, as he innocently shared his music with all his neighbours in the small semi-detached community. Valentine's 'Goodbye' from *Faust*; 'Dead for Bread'. The Ma, who was even closer to this eclectic recital than the neighbours, eventually put it forcefully: 'For God's sake, can you not sing something cheerful?' From then on, the Da interspersed his canon with crowd-pleasing favourites, such as 'The Floral Dance' and 'Me Father Died, I Closed His Eyes Outside the Cabin Door' and 'Goodbye, from the White Horse Inn'. He only ever knew the first couple of lines from 'The Bandolero', which was a blessing. The neighbours never complained, although the ringing tones of the manly baritone were enough to waken the dead, never mind the children in their little beds nearby. Just as well – the Da was a shy man, and would never have sung another note. He sang for himself. But Tom could still hear his voice when he closed his eyes and remembered.

The Pooka

The farmers had come in from the country, never slow to the promise of free food and drink. Usually they would be in their muddy boots on cattle market days, causing the bank porter to mutter darkly about 'bogmen' ruining his polished floor, but Tom knew all too well that the promise of a free ham sandwich at the opening party would bring them running from miles away. What was it about ham sandwiches and the farming community? If it came to that, cream crackers with butter? And the superstitions, the half-believed tales of the 'little people' and their capricious ways . . .

After a year as a junior, the powers that be, who, of course, knew nothing of his bungling incompetence and utter ignorance of even the basics of banking practice, sent Tom as a 'temporary relief' to a little town in the Midlands of Ireland that he'd barely heard of. The usual suspects were in charge: a cynical cashier whose career had stalled, a frustrated assistant manager who thought he should be the boss, and a manager who had been promoted well beyond his abilities, with a card on the inside of his desk that read 'Debit the receiver. Credit the giver'.

Within a couple of days Tom had reduced the book-keeping to chaos, partly through ignorance, but mainly because he couldn't wait to get out of the place. He'd gone to a couple of local 'hops', but the girls treated him like a pariah, because he worked for a 'Protestant' bank.

Tom's digs were rubbish: small bedroom, bath-room down the corridor, and a landlady steeped in the great Irish cookery tradition of vegetables cooked to extinction, meat like the sole of a farmer's boot, and boiled potatoes with everything. What really drove him mad was that the landlady, Maggie, thought that she was a great cook, because of the hypocritical compliments of her paying guests, a husband who lived in fear and trembling of her moods, and another great Irish tradition of nobody ever telling her the truth. It wasn't that she lived in a fantasy world, her life was too hard for that, but like a lot of rural people, old traditions died hard with her; a fast belief in the Catholic Church as the only route to life hereafter was mingled with an older tradition of fairy rings, the magical hare, 'changeling' children, the cunning of the 'little people'. She firmly believed all the local stories about people who had been trapped into their wily, wicked ways and had even confided in Tom about her own experience with one of the little people.

*

Maggie must have imagined it, she thought, as she put the kettle on. Shopping got on her nerves, all that fussing around the town's small supermarket, everybody wanting to chat, when all she wanted was to get home for a nice cup of tea. Her nerves were on edge, that was it. That couldn't have been a tiny little man waving at her, as she turned the corner of the lane that led to the farm. She'd only glimpsed him, it was his long black cloak and hat, or she wouldn't have noticed him at all. Now she wasn't convinced she'd seen anything – wasn't Brendan always accusing her of getting over-excited over nothing, and seeing things that weren't there? She made the tea, and sat back in her favourite kitchen chair with a deep breath. A tiny little man, waving at her. She wouldn't tell Brendan about him, he'd say she'd been at the whiskey. The little people, she thought; her mother used to tell her tales of them and their mischief-making, how they used to steal babies from their cots, and substitute fairy children in their place. They cast spells on you if you offended them and they took offence at the smallest thing. When she was little the fairy stories sometimes kept her from sleeping, but she never really believed them, and now, this little man . . .

Maggie must have dozed off and the knocking on the door made her jump. She got up too quickly, it made her dizzy for a moment, as she went to answer the knocking. When she opened the door, she saw nothing at first, then she looked down, and there he was, her little man. No more than three feet tall including his hat, his cloak reaching the ground, a black beard, pale skin and bright, black eyes.

'Howya, missus,' he said, in a voice too deep for a person of his size. 'Would you have such a thing as a glass of water for a weary traveller?' Before she could answer, he had slipped by her and was in the kitchen. 'Is that a cup of tea you're having, missus? I'd love a cup of tea.' The water in the kettle was still hot, so she made another cup.

'Will you take milk and sugar?'

'Lovely, missus,' he said, as he made himself comfortable in one of the kitchen chairs.

'I haven't seen you around here before,' she said. 'No,' he said, 'very few see me. I'm too small.'

She laughed. 'You are. You're not one of the little people are you, like a leprechaun?'

'Leprechaun!' he sneered. 'Sure they all died out years ago. I'm a Pooka, there's only a few of us left. This is a grand cup of tea.' He sat back in the chair, closed his eyes and fell asleep.

She didn't want to wake him, so she went about her chores as quietly as possible.

The Pooka woke a little later.

'I'm starvin',' he said in his deep voice, 'is there anything to eat at all?'

'There's always plenty to eat in this house,' she replied, offended. 'I'm well known around here for keeping a good table.'

'That's powerful,' he said. 'Do I smell potatoes? I love a potato.'

'There's a few left over from dinner,' she said. The little man rose from the chair. 'Let me at them!' She spooned the last of the left-over potatoes onto a plate, and he climbed nimbly up a chair to sit at the kitchen table, his head just stretching over its top. He'd finished the plate before she'd turned from the stove. 'I suppose you wouldn't have a sup of buttermilk to wash the potatoes down?'

'Why wouldn't I?' she said, pouring him a glass. He downed the drink in one gulp, and sprang from the table with a laugh.

'That's better! A Pooka needs feedin', or we get very ratty.'

'You'll be off then?' she asked. It was getting late, and Brendan would be in, looking for his tea, and she wasn't sure how he would take the little stranger.

'Ah, sure this is grand here, missus,' he said as he settled into his chair. 'I'm in no rush.' And, in the wink of an eye, fell fast asleep again.

There was nothing for it but to start cooking the tea, distractedly looking at the little fellow and wondering what Brendan would say. Brendan said the usual when he came through the door:

'What a day, Maggie, who'd be a farmer?' He took off his boots at the door, rather than drag the dirt of the cow-byre into the house.

'What's for tea? I'll just give me hands a wash in the sink.'

'Rashers and egg,' she said, 'the usual,' with one eye on the little man, to see if the noise had woken him up. But he still seemed fast asleep.

'Any of those potatoes left that we had at dinner time?' asked her husband. 'They were grand. I'd eat a couple with my tea and I'm sure Martin wouldn't mind them when he comes in.' Martin was the farm-hand, who lived in a little cottage down the lane and always had his meals with them. He walked in as they were talking, taking his boots off first. He was big, young and hearty.

'There y'are, missus,' Martin shouted. 'God save all here, barring the cat!'

'Ah, come on, Martin! Our last cat died years ago.'

'Well,' said Martin, 'what's that, sitting in the chair?'

It was a little black cat, to Maggie's astonishment, curled up in the very chair where the Pooka had been sitting. She began to feel faint, and had to lean on the table. Brendan was almost as surprised as she was.

'I never noticed it, when I came in. When did you buy a cat, Maggie, or is it a stray?'

'It just wandered into the house out of the yard today,' Maggie said, glad of the excuse.

'Well,' said Brendan, 'we'll keep it. The barn is overrunning with mice and rats since the last cat died.'

'It might belong to somebody else,' Maggie said, suddenly fearful.

'Sure, who else would it belong to?' said Martin, 'I'm the only neighbour you have for a couple of miles. Anyway, it's been a busy day. Any chance of one of those floury potatoes we had for dinner?'

'I threw those out,' Maggie said, quickly. 'Let me get on, these rashers and eggs won't cook themselves.'

They sat down to tea, but Maggie hardly ate a thing, distractedly looking at the chair with its little black cat, sleeping peacefully. The men hardly noticed, talking of a cow that was about to calve, and as soon as they finished, went out to the byre to check on the animal.

The Pooka got up from the chair the moment the men left. 'That bacon and egg smelled lovely,' he said. 'I suppose there wouldn't be as much as a rasher rind left?' Maggie was speechless. When her senses had recovered, she asked, 'Would you not prefer a saucer of milk?'

'Ah, now, Maggie. Pookas can turn into anything they like – cat, dog, bird, horse. But you know that

I'll always be a Pooka to you and I'll be damned if I'll be chasing mice and rats for that husband of yours and that other eejit. If he annoys me, I'll turn into a bull, and that'll be the end of him.'

'You wouldn't!' she cried, shocked.

'Never cross a Pooka,' he warned. 'But if people are nice to us, it's a different story. Maybe I could cast a spell over that cow that's calving, if there was such a thing as a slice of toast and jam and a cup of tea going?'

The cow calved perfectly, to Brendan's delight, and over the years, crops flourished and life became easier for Maggie. Even Martin took his leave in the end, after his little cottage was suddenly burned to the ground, shortly after he kicked a stray dog that had appeared in the farmyard, a day after the cat disappeared. Martin then moved away to another farm, and Maggie realized that she was relieved.

'I never liked him anyway,' she confessed to the dog, which had wandered into the kitchen. The dog growled, settled into its favourite chair, and fell asleep.

A Christmas Turkey

Tom couldn't believe it when he glanced at his watch, in between sips of the glass of red wine he had taken up – more to have something in his hand than any great wish to drink the stuff, which was the worst he'd tasted since his irreligious swigs at the communion wine when he was an altar-boy. The alternative was the white, which he had tried first, and dumped quickly before it gave him acid indigestion for the rest of his life. He was sure he'd been standing around making small talk to the customers for hours, but they'd flung open the new glass doors at midday, and it was only one o'clock, with no sign of any of the freeloaders taking their leave, either. Why would they? The caterers had just brought in another load of sandwiches. He hoped that they'd be cheese or sardine, that might thin the crowd out, particularly the farmers, but no, the eejits had brought in more ham. They'd be there till Christmas at this rate . . .

*

Those Were the Days

The Christmas Shop was open. Full to bursting with baubles, myriads of crackers, trees a triumph of Yuletide decoration, small but perfectly formed Santas and reindeers, all reassuringly expensive. It was barely September, but it was only a matter of weeks before they switched on the Christmas lights from uptown to downtown, from Grafton Street to Henry Street, and the trumpeting of the January Sales would follow, as night the day.

Tom remembered when the Christmases of his boyhood started; on the train to Dublin at the beginning of Christmas week, on the way with his mother to his granny's and auntie's house in the city's suburbs. He couldn't remember any Christmases of his youth that hadn't been spent that way. He seemed to remember getting a smut in his eye when he looked out of the train's window, and his mother nearly taking a layer of skin off his face with a wet corner of her handkerchief, but it was a memory he apparently shared with everybody, so he wasn't sure after all the years if he'd imagined it and had even come to doubt that he'd ever been on a steam train.

When they got to Granny's, there was the usual fussing by his four aunties and great aunt Mag, who was a French-polisher by trade, and carried a suggestion of it about her. A cup of tea, rashers and egg, and off to bed. He couldn't remember much about the week and the run up to Christmas, except for the pantos that his auntie May took him to, at the Gaiety and the Olympia theatres. The dame at the first was always played by Jimmy O'Dea, and the other by Jack Cruise, the two comedy giants of Dublin theatre in the fifties. Strange, the things that stick in your mind, like the Knickerbocker Glory he was always treated to by his adoring aunt at Cafolla's Ice-Cream Parlour.

The excitement in the house was almost tangible as the big day grew ever closer, his aunts bustling off to work and coming back in the evening exhausted from lugging mysterious parcels down the road from the bus stop.

Everybody stayed up later than usual, even though they had to get up for work in the morning, and hands of whist were played, accompanied by ham sandwiches and fruit cake. There wasn't much alcohol around, drink was more expensive in those days, but the air was heavy with cigarette smoke, and laughter, as her sisters teased Auntie Nelly, the eldest, who took herself and life seriously and rarely saw the funny side of things. She felt she was responsible, particularly for the turkey, since none of her sisters could cook to save their lives.

Tom's father, having fulfilled his responsibility as manager, closed the grocery store on Christmas Eve, and caught the last train to Dublin. The boy was always allowed to stay up until the Da arrived, tired but happy, looking forward to the big day.

In the morning there was a load of presents at the foot of his bed, but early and all as excitement had woken him, he hardly had time to tear the wrappings apart before being forced into his best suit and off to Mass with the family. Nelly, ever conscious of her heavy responsibility, had been to an earlier Mass, and was already up to her armpits with the turkey in the kitchen. Back from Mass and straight into the books and toys – that helped but never quite overcame the boy's anticipation of the great bird whose odours filled the house.

Christmas dinner was always in the kitchen, there wasn't a table big enough in the 'good' room, and Nelly was damned if she was going to break her neck lugging that huge thing up the stairs from the kitchen, having already nearly killed herself cooking it. The Da did the carving, delicately slicing, while everybody paid statutory tribute to a juicy bird and

A Christmas Turkey

Nelly's sterling work at the oven. She always took the accolades with a modest shrug, her only further contribution an admonishment to anyone she saw treating her bird with less than the manners and dignity required, by eating too quickly. 'You're not rushing for a bus!'

Nelly's turkey, like herself, was a well-nourished bird, and cooked to a turn, which was all right by the boy, since the skin, the part he was interested in, was a succulent, crisp delight. When dinner was over, and everybody repaired to the 'good' room for a snooze or a restorative hand of cards, he'd be back in the kitchen, gorging on the skin of the carcass. It led to certain complaints later, along the lines of 'Who's been picking at the turkey?' – particularly as he'd been at the stuffing as well – and cold turkey sandwiches were required as sustenance around the adult card table.

Tom had his share of the sandwiches as well, and occasionally wondered if his inability to resist a plate of sandwiches to this day was rooted in memories of soft white bread, butter and turkey . . .

Christmases have been joyful ever since, and dinners as memorable, since he'd had the sense to marry a queen among women, a mistress of pan and skillet, who not only handles the Big Bird with consummate ease and skill, but who carves like a surgeon as well. It was a skill Tom had never mastered, his father having always taken the knife from his hand, even as an adult, before he hacked the unfortunate turkey to ribbons.

Unlike his long-departed Auntie Nelly, however, the aforesaid queen among women does not hold the Christmas turkey in reverence as a bird apart and above all other avian pretenders. Rather, she regards it as something of an unprepossessing lump, lacking in flavour, with no room for variety of cooking or presentation: 'Boring to cook and to eat.' Weakly, Tom puts his memories of the succulence of boyhood turkey, the skin and the stuffing, aside, in the interests of domestic bliss.

'What about,' says the much-beloved, 'a change this Christmas? A couple of plump pheasants, flavoursome and gamey, in a Bordelaise sauce?'

It didn't seem such a terrible prospect, but you would have thought that he was taking away his children's birthright when they heard the news. 'Pheasant? We always have turkey! It won't be the same without turkey!' Herself gave in, and it's been turkey ever since, which came as a great relief to him. It wouldn't be the same without it, and the very scent of its roasting brought back so many boyhood memories.

For him, Christmas has never been about presents, or trees, or baubles and crackers, reindeer or even Santa Claus. It's always been Auntie Nelly's turkey, that succulent skin, and nobody 'rushing for a bus'.

A Girl Called Nelly

Tom spotted two elderly female customers in the corner of the room, reminding him again of his own maiden aunties, now gone to their eternal reward, but always 'the girls' of affectionate memory.

Nelly was the eldest of the girls, but he had no difficulty remembering all their faces, their characters. He had spent every Christmas, every summer holiday in their little house on a quiet Dublin road. All of his memories in their gentle, kind company were happy ones. But how happy were *they*? He'd never thought to ask. They were the daughters of Frank and 'Muds', their affectionate name for a lovely little mother, whose real name Tom never knew. Frank had been a sergeant-major in a British Army battalion in Ireland, but since Tom had only hazy memories of him, his clearest recollection just a military moustache, he never knew whether his maternal granddad had fought in the Boer War or on the 'wrong side' during the Irish Uprising, and neither

Frank's wife nor his daughters ever referred to his military career. Tom felt a particular affinity with the old boy, who like himself had moved around the country, not from bank to bank, but barracks to barracks, where Frank and Mud's daughters were born. They could all recite the poems of Robert W. Service, 'The Shooting of Dan McGrew' being a particular favourite, and sang 'come-all-yes' around the piano in the 'good' room, when anyone could be found to play it. They all had their own versions of a tale they told of a Christmas years before in a Dublin barracks, when soldiers, wives, families were gathered about a big Christmas tree. Rose, Tom's mother, was lifted up to place the fairy on top of the tree. Afterwards, the army commander's wife approached Muds, and asked, since she and her husband were childless, and Muds and Frank had five daughters, if they could adopt Rose. The kind offer, which would have alleviated the financial strain on Frank and Muds, was refused. The girls forever afterwards loved to speculate how different Rose's life would have been, if the commander's wife's offer had been accepted, for the officer's new command was in India. Tom often wondered how he would have made out, as a son of the Raj.

The girls didn't go out to work, they 'went out to business'. Work was for the lower orders, shop assistants and hawkers on Moore Street. Nelly and May, Kitty, Rose and Dinah were a cut above, particularly now that they were living in their Auntie Mag's house on Clonliffe Road, Drumcondra, the acme of Dublin middle-class respectability.

The three elder girls remained virgins all their lives, only Rose and Dinah ever marrying. It was the way it was then, the population of eligible adult males having been decimated by the Great War. And Nelly, May and Kitty weren't the kind of raving beauties that had a procession of mooning eejits knocking on the door. So Nelly cycled to 'business' every morning, to the curtain department of Dublin's grandest store, Clery's, rumoured to have been once owned and named by a descendant of Napoleon's great love, Désirée Clary – Clery's being the Irish translation of Clary's. You could believe that if you wanted to, it made very little difference to anyone in the curtain department. May, who smoked like a chimney, eschewed the bike and took the bus from the top of the road to a Catholic bookshop in Dublin named Veritas, where she had risen to manager, and was entrusted to peruse incoming popular fiction for even the slightest suggestion of filth. The merest hint of hanky-panky and it was goodbye to the author's chances of sharing the shelves of Veritas along with Thomas à Kempis, and the Acts of the Apostles. G. K. Chesterton barely made the cut, and only because he was a Catholic, although an English one.

Kitty was a problem: perhaps a little slower on the uptake than the rest of the family, she left school even earlier than the others, and was apprenticed to a French-polisher, her Aunt Mag's trade. How Aunt Mag had managed to acquire a desirable property in Drumcondra, even given consummate skills in French-polishing, remained a mystery that she carried to the grave, along with her virginity. Another good woman spared the indignity of relations with men, who as Nelly once forcefully put it, 'were only after the one thing'. To which her younger sister, Rose, newly wed, tartly riposted, 'And how would you know?'

In later life, Kitty was knocked down by a car while crossing the road, and never really got over it – coming back to consciousness in hospital to see a black doctor leaning over her. Black people or any other colour than pale pink and freckled were a rare sight indeed in Dublin then, so there was some excuse for poor Kitty. She never went back to the

French-polishing, and remained in her bed, her immaculately buffed and painted nails peeking over the coverlet. She'd had enough of the stained yellow fingers of her trade.

Rose and Dinah went to business by bicycle, working at the same grocery store. Not behind the counter, of course, but in the book-keeping department. The men that they married both worked behind the counter, but a man was a man, and at a time of male shortage even a respectable girl from Drumcondra couldn't be too particular, although a couple of grocer's curates were hardly the cream of the crop. Muds didn't care, two out of five wasn't bad – as long as the fellas spoke up, because she was as deaf as a post, with a hearing aid that screeched like a banshee when she turned it up. She could cook, but it was a skill she'd only managed to pass on to Nelly – the others couldn't boil water.

Nelly and May contented themselves with lady friends, one of whom upset the apple cart by getting a boyfriend, and married, late in life. Nelly's friend was another Nelly, a fine lump of a woman, with a military bearing, who would only drink water when invited to tea at Clonliffe Road, and always insisted 'let the tap run' when offered a glass. She was probably right, the taps were as full of lead as the pipes of Dublin's pubs were full of a hundred years of sludge, giving the pint of stout its legendary weight and distinctive flavour. 'You can't beat the pint you get in Dublin.'

The two Nellies sought the far horizons, trekking together to foreign fields such as the Isle of Man and London. In 1937, they flew bravely in the face of convention, and Frank Byrne, by journeying to Germany. Frank, who was no eejit, had heard what was going on in Germany at the time, and came out strongly against his daughter travelling to a country where there was persecution of the Jews. Not for any moral reason, he just thought that Nelly's dark looks might get her into trouble. Scorning all warnings, the girls took off for the Rhineland, where they were well enough received to be invited to a great Nazi rally, at which the main speaker was Hitler's confidante, Martin Bormann. The jolly evening was ruined for the girls when some deluded gobdaw took a pot-shot at Bormann, and the rally disintegrated. Nonetheless the girls came back with a very positive impression of German life under the Third Reich, to which the Irish equivalent apparently compared very unfavourably. The admired Germans' attempt at world domination effectively scuppered any further wide-ranging travel plans for the next ten years as far as the Nellies were concerned. The bigger Nelly died, possibly from lead poisoning, Muds and Frank went to their eternal reward, then Nelly and May, inevitably done in by the fags. Kitty, always frail, couldn't live without them, and now they're all buried together, in a cemetery with a lovely view of Dublin Bay. Sad, uneventful, unfulfilled lives? The Byrne sisters had their place in the world, important to them. And like every individual ever born, there has never been, and never will be, anybody like them again . . .

Johnny the Chancer

Tom looked more closely at the couple of old biddies
on their own, widow women, who, in common with
the usual way of the world, had outlived their husbands, sipping, which was all that was possible, at
their white wine, while making short work of the egg
and cress sandwiches. Although they hardly knew
each other, they found plenty to talk about: huddling
together for warmth, Tom thought, more at home
cackling around a cauldron. He should have ordered
sherry for the ladies, he realized, and maybe some
scampi from the chippie. This crowd would eat anything, after a couple of drinks. He could murder a
pint himself, this minute. Why did that remind him
of his late pal Johnny? Maybe it was because they'd
had their first Guinness together, brazening it out in
the pub at seventeen. He'd just joined the bank as a
junior, and to his great relief hadn't been sent for
his first posting to some hole down the country, but a
Dublin branch. Johnny would come in every week to

cash his wages, one of the few customers of his own age, and over the weeks they struck up a rapport.

Johnny was a 'character', always saw the funny side of things, always ready for a laugh. As the green-grocer round the corner droned on into one ear, with the manager of the post office occupying his other one, Tom allowed himself a secret smile at the memory of his friend, as both of them 'did a runner' without paying the bill from an expensive, at least by their standards, restaurant. Out the door, down the street they went, laughing. They weren't being followed, they stopped to catch their breath, and then Johnny groaned, 'Oh no! I've left me good raincoat behind! The Ma'll kill me. I've got to go back and get it!' And he did, walking back into the restaurant, sitting down at the same table from which they had lately decamped. The waiter, who'd watched the early escape, was surprised. 'You're back?'

'Of course,' said the bold Johnny, 'what do you think I am, a chancer? I'll have a cup of coffee to finish.' Even as the waiter disappeared into the kitchen, Johnny was on his feet, into the cloakroom, raincoat over his arm, and breathlessly back on the street.

Johnny wasn't stupid, but he hated the Christian

Brothers and left school to be apprenticed to a plumber. His father was a policeman, with enough contacts to get him into a trade, but it was his mother who was responsible for his character, and his sense of humour. He was precocious in his pursuit of women, but from Irish romantic time immemorial it was a lucky man who had ever got more than a kiss – without tongues. He got good at that, and boasted that a woman once said to him, 'Kiss me, Johnny, till I faint.' His technique was to laugh women into his arms, but once he got them there, he had a tendency to blow it, because, like all comedians, he would sacrifice anything for a laugh.

A great story-teller in a nation in which every dog and devil thinks that they can tell a tale, he could hold a room in thrall with his racy yarns, and loved to watch the shocked expressions on the faces of the not-all-that innocent girls that he had lured into his clutches as he recounted one of his favourites, 'Yellow Boots'.

The story is about a man and woman who are naked in bed together. She's disappointed. 'Your auld man is very droopy this evening.'

'I know,' he says proudly, 'he's lookin' at me new yellow boots.' The lady thinks about it, then says,

'Well it's a pity you didn't get a new yellow hat, while you were at it.'

This was tame by Johnny's usual standards but not something that was ever going to get him past a 'coort'. He never cared, he always laughed long before he got to the punch-line of his own jokes; nobody enjoyed them more.

Johnny married a lovely girl, who had heard all his jokes a thousand times before, but still laughed at every one as if hearing it for the first time. His best jokes were at his own expense, and his family's. Blessed with hair like a lavatory-brush, he kept his unruly locks firmly in place with a daily smothering of Brylcreem, but his hair took on a life of its own at bedtime, and Johnny had regular recourse to one of his sister's hairnets to calm its wildness. It wasn't something that a man of the world would want the world to know. Unfortunately, his friends called around when he was having a lie-in one Saturday, and his mother showed them up to his room, and the rest is the kind of slur that a sensitive soul carries to the grave. He still couldn't resist telling the story, which pre-empted some, if not all, of his friends' steady jeering.

In his drinking, as in his life, there was no

half-measure; he went for it. One Christmas Eve, having downed the regulation excessive traditional festive cups of cheer, he thought that he'd better make his way home, rather than spend the holy holiday in the care of the Gardai on a drunk and disorderly charge. In those innocent, careless days when drink-driving was an accepted part of Irish life, and Dublin wasn't in the permanent traffic gridlock it is these days, Johnny somehow remembered where he'd put his car keys, and even where he'd parked the car. Negotiating the narrow streets of the Fair City, he was well on his way up the incline just before Baggot Street Bridge, when he decided to dispense with the remains of a Christmas cigar that had come to the end of its natural life. As with all of his cars, there was a minor fault: this one had a window on the driver's side that wouldn't wind down. Keeping his eye on the road, and driving at a safe pace up the hill, Johnny opened the door of the car, and hurled the cigar butt out onto the road. Unfortunately, his judgement being a tad befuddled by the demon drink, he hurled himself out of the car door along with his dead cigar. As Johnny sprawled on the road, he watched as his car slid back down the hill, gathering pace as it went, banging into several other parked vehicles as it careered on, before being brought to a merciful halt by the pavement.

He staggered to his feet and ran down the hill after his runaway car, clambered in, and, his head slightly clearer, drove with all speed the rest of the way home. As he came through his front door, he was heard to say, 'Quick! The boys in blue are after me!' before collapsing onto the settee and falling into a deep sleep.

Cars were never a strong point with him. He drove all the way to the Costa Blanca in Spain in a Fiat Uno: Dublin then ferry to Liverpool, Liverpool to Dover, ferry to Calais, Calais to Calpe. Taking the plane seemed to him the coward's way out. The little thing gave up the ghost shortly after Calpe and he left it in the hands of a small local garage. When he eventually got back to Dublin, grudgingly taking a plane, he would phone the Spanish garage every week to find out how things were going with his little car. Nobody seemed to know anything about it, possibly because they didn't speak a word of English and he couldn't put two words together in Spanish. Every so often he would tell Tom that he was going down to Spain to straighten things out once and for all, but his unfortunate accident with a hired caravan distracted him. He'd hired it to take his little family on seaside trips, but on the very first one he took it under a particularly low-slung bridge. The roof of the bridge ripped the top off the caravan. Despite all Johnny's efforts, the owner couldn't see the funny side, and Johnny and his family took the bus to the seaside for a long time after that.

His mother, from whom he inherited an aristocratic nose, long legs, and a taste for the finer things in life that always seemed just out of grasp, liked a hand of cards and a convivial evening, and Johnny loved to regale a small crowd with a tale of an evening after a card game when she was walking home with her fellow gamblers, including his sister, a bit of a demon at the poker in her own right. It was his sister who told him that as his mother walked along, she broke wind loudly, and immediately turned to the companion nearest her, and apologized, 'Sorry, Rory, I beg your pardon.' According to Johnny's sister, Rory's gracious reply caused her to cling to nearby railings wetting herself with laughter.

'Ah, sure no bother on you, Mrs T. The gun's your own.'

Johnny's long gone now, but he took a bright light with him.

The Producer

Old Hanratty had made his way across the crowded room and was now standing at Tom's side; he was a friendly fellow and the type of man who was always eager to talk of days gone by. Old Hanratty was the cashier when Tom arrived as a junior at the Cattle Market branch, now transformed into a glass-framed modern edifice. Hanratty had been a decent old sod, good-humoured enough for someone who was never going to achieve the golden dream of managership, and he was in no way resentful now of the little twerp who had shambled into the branch all those years ago, without an idea, and was now the manager. Hanratty had a firm hold of Tom's sleeve, reminiscing with the benefit of a couple of glasses of the demon drink, about a golden era of banking life that had never existed.

'I remember the first day you arrived, and I thought, he can't be as big an eejit as he looks. I was wrong!' Hanratty exploded into laughter. 'And what about little Katie? What did you and her get up to in the safe, eh?' Tom smiled, and nodded in apparent agreement, but only because he wanted to leave the old boy with his fantasies, and couldn't be bothered telling him the truth. Katie, blonde, vivacious, was like a breath of fresh air in the dreary fug of the old bank, but her romantic ambitions extended far beyond the realms of a mere bank clerk.

In those days, with a surprising regard for its customers, the bank threw its portals open on a Saturday for a couple of hours. It wasn't the only concession: staff were allowed to wear their club blazers, a major gesture to liberal thinking, for any Irishman could tell your religion immediately by looking at the crest on your blazer. As soon as the bank closed, it was off to the rugby club, into the team colours and onto the pitch, whatever the weather. The showers wouldn't have been out of place in Mountjoy Jail, so many didn't bother; anyway, it was eating into drinking time. Into the blazer, off to the club bar, and the reviving pint. Or several, before it was considered appropriate to beg a lift in a friend's car, and off to one of the many Saturday night tennis-/rugby-club 'hops'. He often saw the lovely Katie there, but apart from a friendly smile, she was frying other poor fish.

Tom wondered where Katie was now. He'd long since lost track of her, after she'd gone to London in search of bigger fish. He smiled at the thought of her laughing face and flirty ways. Tom thought he could have done with her there today. And Steve.

Steve was another who'd taken the Mail Boat to fame and fortune. They had spent a month in the bank's training school, learning how to separate half-crowns from florins, and how to count bank-notes with the left hand, apparently a skill vouchsafed only to the best of bank clerks. Steve and he hit it off immediately, their bond strengthened by copious draughts of Guinness, and fried egg and chips later in the Bankers' Club to sober up and set the world to rights.

They'd both joined the bank because they hadn't wanted to put their parents to further expense with three or more years at university, getting a useless degree. Except that Steve hadn't stopped learning. Three evenings a week after work, he studied for a City and Guilds qualification as a sound technician. He didn't want to be in the bank forever, and unlike others did something about it. He'd always wanted to work in radio, and when he qualified, he applied for, and got, a job with R.E. – the Irish national radio station. But that wasn't the height of his ambition. He'd grown up listening to British radio stations, and London was where he wanted to be. After a couple of years' experience, he got a job there as a technical operator. After a few years more, Steve had moved on to production. He came back home to see his family and friends every year to bask in their congratulations and always revelled in the tale of when he had gone into his old bank branch, by now an established producer, and cashed a cheque with a teller who had worked with him there.

'How ya?' asked the teller. 'Do you remember Mick who worked here with you? He's just made cashier in Letterkenny. You know, you left the bank at the wrong time.'

*

Steve didn't exactly pinch himself every morning when he woke up but he knew that, apart from Ringo Starr, he was the luckiest man in the world. A producer on the radio, with his own table at Wheeler's every lunchtime, with the waiters knowing his name, and the chef preparing the Sole Mornay without him even having to order. And it wasn't costing him or the radio company a penny. Well of course there was an unspoken kick-back to the record-plugger who was footing the bill; it didn't seem an awful imposition to include the plugger's record on the play-list of the daily radio show he was producing. He didn't feel guilty: it was the way things were done, even the gifts of a hamper at Christmas, or a bottle of single malt every so often, and nothing compared to the perks of the executive producers. At least he came into work every morning, and prepared the week's programmes. The execs turned up just before lunch, and were never seen again afterwards, unless a record company was hosting a table at the White Tower, or Ronnie Scott's.

When lunches and dinners were not considered sufficient incentive for a spin on a popular show, sex was also on offer, but he had no problems in that area, thank you very much. It was too much like paying for it and he'd never needed to do that. He had been about sixteen, and delivering on his bicycle for the local grocer to keep himself in pocket money, when he realized that he had a way with women. It was a surprise and delight to find how many housewives welcomed him in for a cup of tea and a little chat on his daily round. Sometimes more than tea and chocolate digestives was on offer, but he wasn't pushed. It was enough that they melted at his smile and admired his blue eyes. That was the way it was as he moved to manhood, too. Sure, sex was okay, but what he sought was adoration. Love 'em and leave 'em, or just leave 'em, as long as they always remembered the smile and the eyes. He wanted women to think of him in their quiet moments of recollection as a romantic, unattainable ideal, who flitted through their lives leaving just an occasional ache for what might have been.

On top of Steve's commitments at the bank and doing his City and Guilds, his father had pulled a few Masonic strings and got him occasional work at a TV studio. He loved it, even the fighting off of the advances of a particularly persistent gay comedian, while enjoying the occasional swooning of female dancers. It was a besotted female TV producer who had shown him the advertisement for his first job in radio.

Steve was called for an interview with a man of military bearing, an old hand who took an immediate liking to him, put a rough soldierly hand on his knee, and gave him the job without checking whether he was qualified. And here he was, a couple of years later, producing a major daily radio show on a national broadcasting network, living off the fat of the land, and everybody, including himself, out to lunch.

His radio show, like the rest of the network, was going from strength to strength; what could go wrong? And then the roof fell in – a tabloid reporter had started to nose around in the murky waters of rumoured 'sex for plays', and within days, the print media were on the trail of scandal like ravening wolves.

It could only end one way, and it did. Badly. Sex orgies colourfully described, participating disc-jockeys and producers named and shamed. The company sought to cleanse the Augean stables with all dispatch: beloved presenters, household names, were ordered to pack their bags; producers, respect-able family men all, had until Big Ben struck midday to clear their desks, and go.

The great Payola scandal waxed fiercely for weeks, but the show had to go on. Daily radio shows wouldn't make themselves and, untouched by any suggestion of sexual indiscretion, he went about his business as usual, only with slightly greater fervour, as heads rolled about him. Luckily, the tabloids had concentrated on 'sex for plays' as much more headline-worthy than 'hospitality for plays', so he and the others who had merely been fed and watered at the record companies' expense were in the clear. But even executives, whose whole lives were changed utterly, with the sad prospect of the canteen for lunch, and hamper-less Christmases, knew that the good times were a changin'.

Steve missed the fine food and wine, but joined the other producers in the pub at lunchtime when he could decently leave the studio. The barmaid responded well to his smile, and flirted satisfactorily. But even in his cups, he knew things had changed, and he felt that he needed some change too. He'd flirted and left them wanting more for too long. He felt he wanted the warmth, the security, of something more permanent.

Steve met her in the club, a secretary, married with two children. She didn't look wistfully at him like the others, but straight in the eye. He found himself, for the first time, seeking the approval and affection of a woman. She told him that she was unhappy in her marriage, and ready for a new relationship. He sold his old flat in London and got a mortgage for a little house in the country, where they could both live the family life, and be happy ever after. He felt he was the happiest he'd ever been, until she told him that she wasn't leaving her husband and family, and after all, hadn't it been fun while it lasted? On the rebound, he married someone that nobody else liked, and it ended after about a year. He agreed to hand over the house to her because he couldn't be bothered with all the fuss, and rented a flat in Shepherd's Bush.

Every so often, an old friend from a record company would invite him out to lunch for old times' sake, no strings attached, but the waiters were indifferent, didn't know him by name any more, and the Sole Mornay was off the menu.

The Feather

Tom made his way around the room, stopping to chat to customer after customer, before finally managing to take a few minutes to refill his drink. As he did, he overheard two middle-aged women gossiping together. They were talking of the Christmas gone by and the sad fate that had befallen one of the local women.

*

She saw it floating gently down, as she pushed the pram along, before it landed at her feet. Rather than walk over it, she stopped and picked it up. It was so white, so flawless, she instinctively ran her fingers gently along the feather to remove any dust from the road. She hadn't much experience of feathers, apart from the one in that ridiculous little 'fascinator' hat she'd worn for her sister's wedding the other year, but this one felt different: firm, but soft, even when she brushed her fingers against the grain. She waved it in front of little Matthew in the pram, and tickled the tip of his nose, and he smiled, just as he always did, at everybody and everything. He reached for the feather, she let him take it and he immediately put it in his mouth. She thought he'd tire of it, just as he usually got fed up with his soother, and expected it to be thrown from the pram. But it was still in his hands when she wheeled the pram through the front door. She tried to take the feather from him as she lifted him out and put him sitting in his high chair, but he clung tightly to it.

Matthew slipped away from life that night as quietly and gently as he had entered, two years before, without a cry. Ever since he'd been born with a serious heart defect, she had dreaded the inevitable day when Matthew would leave her. The doctor had called him 'a brave little fella' for clinging on to life when he hadn't been expected to live beyond a week. Every day she'd prayed for a miracle, every morning when she woke rushing to the cot, hoping for some sign of recovery. She let the feather drop from her hands over Matthew's grave, and turned quickly away before they covered it with earth.

The house was heavy with grief, even with the family and friends who'd come to mourn and console her and she felt an ungrateful relief when they all left, with assurances of love and support. She felt more alone than she had ever been, even as a pregnant single woman. Now, a single mother without a child in an empty house, with Christmas only a week away. Forget that, she wasn't going to celebrate the birth of a baby all those years ago in Bethlehem, when her own had been taken away to join Him in Heaven. She felt a wave of resentment, a hatred of life and a cruel God, and she cried. It felt as if she'd been crying for years, an endless sobbing that lingered always in the back of her throat.

She didn't feel as if she'd slept a wink, but the ring on the door woke her with a start. She pulled on a dressing gown, and sleepily made her way downstairs to her front door. She opened it, expecting the postman or the scatty young one from a couple of doors down, who was always running out of milk or sugar for her kids' breakfasts, but there was nobody there. She thought that she must have been dreaming, and had imagined the ringing of the doorbell. Nobody on the road outside her little front garden, either. She went into the kitchen and made herself a cup of tea, and took it back upstairs while she got dressed. She wanted to go into the little room as she had for the last two years to check the baby in his cot, but she forced herself to go downstairs again. She had a job to go to, a living to make, although it all seemed pointless now.

For just a second, she wondered what was keeping May, who looked after Matthew when she went out to work, and then the ache in her throat started again, and she had to sit down in the kitchen until the weeping stopped. Now she was late, and was going to miss the bus to town. She rushed out of the front door, and nearly trod on the feather that she hadn't noticed when she'd opened the door earlier. She picked it up, put it in her pocket, and ran for her bus. Everyone was really understanding at the office, and the boss had called her in privately to offer his sympathies and her Christmas bonus. It seemed much bigger than last year, but she wasn't going to complain.

She was in a better mood as she turned the corner of the cul-de-sac in which she lived, and then her heart leapt in shock to see her house was draped in Christmas lights, and the lights of a Christmas tree were shining through her front window. She opened the gate, and made her way under the twinkling lights to her front door. For some reason she didn't feel nervous as she turned the key in the lock, and stepped inside. The house felt warm and welcoming, and she smelled the pine of the tree before she opened the door of the front room to look at it, bemused. She felt her spirits lift even as she tried to make sense of it all: the lights, the tree, the different feel of the house, her own feelings of giddiness, as if the weight that had been bearing down on her was lifted.

She took off her coat, and felt something in the pocket. She'd forgotten about the feather that she had picked up from the doorstep that morning, rushing for the bus. It was white and flawless, and she suddenly remembered the last feather, the one Matthew had so stubbornly held on to. The lightness of her mood changed at the memory. She sat and looked at the Christmas tree for a few minutes, then turned off its lights, and made her way upstairs to bed. She couldn't help but look into Matthew's little room and his empty cot. It was then that she realized that she'd been holding tightly on to the white feather. She let it drop gently into the cot, just as she had let the first feather drop into the little boy's grave.

Her sleep was full of dreams of Matthew, happy

and smiling, and when the doorbell woke her again, she felt brighter than the morning before as she went downstairs. Nobody there again, but another white feather, sitting on a large hamper. This time, she didn't bother looking up and down the road to see who had rung the bell, she knew that no one was there. It wasn't easy carrying the big hamper into her kitchen, and it was only when she had opened it, and taken out the ham, turkey, cake, biscuits, chocolates and all the other Christmas goodies that she realized that the white feather must have fallen off the top, but she suddenly knew not to look for it, as she emptied the hamper and began to plan the feast that had, only yesterday, been the furthest thing from her mind. She went into the front room to turn on the Christmas tree lights, but they were already shining merrily, as were the even more mysterious lights that shone over her front door. It was Saturday, she didn't have to run for the bus, so she took a cup of tea back up to her bedroom. Once again she looked into Matthew's little room. The feather she had dropped in the cot was no longer there.

Her mother rang for the first time in ages, sounding sad and apprehensive, to invite her to join the family for Christmas Day, but she insisted over her mother's astonished protests that everyone come to her for lunch, saying that she had enough to feed an army, she hadn't done Christmas for years and it was about time she put Nigella's recipes to the test. The doorbell rang again, but this time it was her neighbours, who had been surprised and pleased by her lights and the tree in her window, and came bearing mince pies newly baked that morning. She welcomed them in, and they ate the warm pies with the wine from the hamper. She hadn't smiled, let alone laughed, for so long.

On Christmas Eve, she went to Midnight Mass. As she made her way home, she wasn't surprised when a flawless white feather drifted from above to land at her feet. She picked it up, stroked it and carried it home. She put it by her bedside table, yet it wasn't there when she woke up – but then she hadn't expected it to be.

The family – her mother and father, younger brother and sister – obviously didn't know what to expect from her on Christmas Day, but her happy mood calmed their fears, as they exchanged presents around the tree, which they agreed was a beauty, drank the mulled wine she'd concocted, and proclaimed Nigella's turkey and trimmings a total triumph. As they left, they said it was the best Christmas ever, and her mother kissed her and said how much they all missed Matthew.

As she waved them off, she half expected a feather to drift slowly down, but then, she realized that if she ever saw another feather, it would be only that of some passing bird.

The Widda

The sandwiches were now thin on the ground, the wine glasses less frequently refilled, the crowd beginning to disperse, to Tom's relief. Good old James and Sinead would be clinging to the wreckage to the last; they'd have to be shovelled out by brute force, and the women were still chatting nine to the dozen in the corner, particularly Mrs Bourke, a cheerful woman who seemed to have blossomed in widowhood. He remembered that on the rare occasions that they both came into the bank, she seemed in the shadow of her late husband. Nowadays, she seemed to know exactly where she was going.

*

For the first year after Joseph died, people couldn't do enough. Friends invited her to dinner, the family either phoned or came around on a regular basis, a male acquaintance even asked her to partner him for the mixed foursomes at the golf club. Everyone was very considerate and sympathetic to a woman on her own.

It didn't last. A couple of years on, and it was just a weekly bridge game and the occasional lunch with her fellow widows. There were no phone calls from those with whom she and Joseph had played golf every Friday, and she couldn't be bothered going all the way to the club and putting her name down for competitions. She couldn't be bothered, either, cooking the way she used to when Joseph was alive. He loved his food, and a couple of glasses of wine at dinner, but it depressed her to sit down and eat on her own at the table every day, so she usually had a cup of tea and a sandwich in front of the television. She watched a lot more television in the daytime now, chat in the mornings, quizzes in the afternoons.

Her friends at lunch and bridge said she looked really well, and 'hadn't she lost a bit of weight?'

Mrs Bourke certainly wasn't going to let her appearance slip; she was always smartly dressed, fully made up, hair done once a week. The house was spotless, and the girls always remarked on it, when it was her turn to host the bridge game. She went to great trouble with the tea and cake on these occasions, her scones with jam and clotted cream freely complimented over the cards.

Her daughter, Eileen, came to see her once a week, and brought her kids. They always lifted her spirits, but the amount of clearing up she had to do after they'd gone exhausted her, and made her wonder how she had managed to bring up her own two kids.

Her son and his three children came to visit less regularly, and she didn't look forward to seeing them as much. Not the kids, they were lovely and growing up so fast. It was just that David, her son, always wanted to talk about her health and, more particularly, money. Had she enough to support herself, was Dad's pension from the bank sufficient? She really didn't want to talk about it, especially when he started in with his usual stuff about the house, the cost of running it, its size, and would she not think of down-sizing to a smaller place, or better again, selling up and moving to one of those luxurious care homes, where everything would be done for her, and she wouldn't need to cook or clean?

It always depressed her. She knew that David meant well, and it probably made sense, but she didn't want to think about leaving the home that she and Joseph had lived in together for nearly forty years. Her son said that material things weren't important, all that counted was her health and comfort. He was wrong: the house and everything in it was more important than anything else in her life. Every room, every piece of furniture, every plate, cup and glass in the cupboard, every picture, every carpet, even the wallpaper, carried memories of the life she and Joseph had built together.

The garden, with its memories of Joseph on the sit-on mower cutting the grass, imagining himself driving Formula One at Brands Hatch. The vegetable patch, which always made his back ache, and produced enough lettuce each year to keep every one of their friends and neighbours in salads for the year. And the rhubarb. She was sure that those to whom Joseph proudly donated much of his bumper crop dumped it in the bin as soon as he was out of their gates.

How could she even think of leaving her entire life behind? Without her things about her, and the memories they carried with them, what was there that made her life worth living? The family and friends she saw less and less frequently, the dinner and golf invitations that had dried up? No, she wasn't moving. Her health was fine, the doctor said she was like a forty-year-old, she drove the car to the bank, the restaurant and the supermarket without a bother.

She often talked to Joseph as if he were still there, wondering what he would do in her situation; and her widowed friends, all coping with loneliness, all of them, as she said, 'just treading water'. What were they waiting for? No knight in shining armour was going to gallop up and sweep them away, there was 'no sign', as she said herself, 'of Omar Sharif coming for her through the desert haze on his camel'. And not a word from George Clooney. Not that she'd consider another man in her life; she'd been so used to Joseph all those years, she'd never get used to another man's ways, his socks, his underwear, ironing his shirts, his personal habits. Over the years she'd got used to Joseph breaking wind in bed, snoring, dragging mud from the garden all over the carpet, hogging the television remote, coming back from the pub the worse for drink and slurring words of love before collapsing into the sofa and falling asleep. It would take her years to adjust to the irritants of a new man, and then, there would be the sex thing. Old fellas on Viagra, trying to recapture their lost youth. Forget it, she knew she couldn't cope with that at all.

And all that rubbish about older women and younger men. 'Cougars', the Americans called them, shameless in their pursuit of toy boys. Take off your clothes, dance around a pole in front of a crowd of drunks, and you're no longer a shameless hussy. Now, you're 'empowered'. Her fellow widows had no idea what that meant, and didn't want to. What really worried them, and what they rarely confronted, were their final years, sitting on their own in a room in the dreaded 'Home', waiting, just waiting.

David and Eileen were surprised when their mother said she was going on a cruise. David thought it a waste of money, but had no argument when she told him the price: 'Three thousand pounds, the cost of two weeks in a rest home, for two weeks in the Mediterranean.' Eileen drove her to Southampton, nagging her the whole journey about being careful of strange men, drinking and over-eating. Two weeks later, she picked a different woman up at Southampton Docks.

Her mother was sparkling with excitement, with tales of life on board the great liner; a comfy cabin with a porthole, and a steward to cater for her every whim. Huge menus, delicious food and wine, lounges to view the sea, dancing, entertainment, and charming people with whom to share a table, a hand of cards, a drink. No tipping, everything included in the price.

'I've booked already for next month,' she said, 'three weeks to South Africa and back. Really exciting!' Eileen remained speechless for the journey home, barely listening to her mother's elated description of her voyage. David tried to reason with his mother when he heard, but she was adamant. 'Next month South Africa, next year the world! I'll be off on a round the world trip, three months of the comfort you've always wanted for me, and I've never felt better in my life.'

'But we'll never see you,' said Eileen.

'But I don't see much of you as it is,' she replied. 'And we'll get together in between my voyages. Though I'm off on another holiday after I've travelled around the world.'

'What's that?'

'It's a ski holiday.'

'The Swiss Alps?'

'No,' she laughed: 'Spending the Kids' Inheritance. Wish me bon voyage.'

A Tale of Two Cars

The party was definitely starting to wane now and a few customers were beginning to depart. Tom glanced out of the glass doors and saw one of the wealthier customers getting into a flashy red sports car. Tom liked his cars but had never quite managed to buy the Mercedes he'd always wanted. Still, he'd had some decent cars in his time, unlike his old friend Dennis . . .

Dennis had two cars parked outside his front gate, both bought for a song from a pal with a garage, and neither worth tuppence. One battered vehicle had a flat battery that he occasionally had the children, or a friend, push, while he turned on the ignition and crashed the gears, in a futile attempt to get the old banger going.

A friend of his wife, who had come for tea, was persuaded to help in the great Get the Austin Cambridge Moving project, by the simple expedient of driving her car gently into the back of the ancient

Austin, thereby moving it forward sufficiently for the crippled old engine to catch fire. Unfortunately, the good woman's car, coming from the top of a small incline, picking up speed, crashed into the back of Dennis's static machine. The collision certainly moved it forward a couple of yards, but rendered the lady's vehicle equally corpsed. For a short time, his home boasted not two, but three apparently knackered cars outside his front door . . .

Dennis looked upon them with an amused pride. After all, the one he drove to work every morning was still a runner. If you can call something that leaked oil like a sieve and coughed its way into town every morning, a 'runner'. His children looked like he did, scruffy but happy. Most of the furniture in the house looked like an explosion in a mattress factory, but everyone behaved with a cheery disregard for the conventions of gracious living. It was open house to any friend passing by in need of a cup of tea, or a heart-starting drop of the hard stuff, and the front door only closed just before everybody went to bed. It was love and life that counted, and in those days, nobody gave a tinker's curse what anybody looked like, and certainly not the state of their motor cars.

Farmers were known to go to market with livestock as big as a calf on the back seat, and smaller animals in the boot, the boot lock inevitably broken but usually tied fairly securely with the indispensable hairy twine that served well to tie the farmer's own boots and as a belt to hold a disreputable raincoat together; in many cases, it was only the dirt that was holding the car together. The Irish attitude to motorized transport was epitomized by an incident reported in a local paper of police stopping a car on a country road, because, even by the standards of the time, it was being driven in an eccentric manner. When the policeman had a look inside, he found two kitchen chairs where the front seats used to be. After exhaustive questioning, the driver, who was sober and had no idea what all the fuss and bother was about, explained that, finding the car seats a great deal more comfortable than the hard old chairs in his kitchen, had taken them out, placed them in front of the kitchen fire, and simply put the kitchen chairs in their place. He said that apart from sliding about a bit on corners, he was comfortable driving, but not as comfortable as he was sitting in front of his kitchen fire.

Nobody with any sense or self-respect bought a new car, or drove around on anything other than rethread tyres. After the pubs closed, they drove, the drink lapping up against their back teeth, for just another pint, and maybe a drop of the hard stuff, to pubs outside the city limits, called 'bona fides', which were not subject to restrictions of opening or closing hours. On most days of the week, and particularly the weekend, drivers, their passengers and anybody foolish enough to take to a country road with or without a light on their bike, freely took their lives in their hands in pursuit of the demon drink . . .

Back to the city in time for early Mass on Sunday morning down by the quays, with the good Father Flanagan, known as 'Flash', who would have a Mass done and dusted in twenty minutes, and you're back home in the bed still smelling of stout, but without waking up your mother, to sleep it off, your religious duties done, and ready for a reviving pint down the pub later.

It wasn't Dennis's way; he'd been a family man too long. And he liked to eat when he drank, usually in Madigan's pub. Nobody could strip a chicken leg like Dennis . . . For more formal dining, he favoured the Acropolis, a little place down a side street that was owned by a Greek who'd never heard of feta cheese, moussaka, or stuffed vine leaves, but did a pretty decent lasagne. The staff at the Acropolis were neither Greek nor Italian, but native-born Irishmen, who, like any of their race, regarded themselves as good as any man, and were not natural-born waiters. Any delay over selecting from the wine-list was usually met by the waiter's impatient 'and what will it be for booze?' They served you a bit like air stewardesses, as if they were doing you a favour . . . Dennis was always suspicious of the obsequious, and preferred places where no one called him 'sir'. He liked pubs where barmen called him by his first name, and greeted him with 'The usual?' He loved to recount a tale of the upmarket travellers, lost in the dark little roads of the west of Ireland, and hungry for their dinner, who, when all hope was lost, and a lonely death of starvation staring them in the face, suddenly came across the lights of a hostelry. Their knock on the door was greeted by a young woman, whose greeting was not in the best traditions of far-famed Irish hospitality, but who opened the door wide enough for the two hungry travellers to enter, and upon being asked if dinner was being served, led them into a simple dining room with chequered oil-cloths on the three or four tables and a stuffed salmon over the hearth, in which struggled the dying remains of what couldn't have been much of a fire in the first place.

'What would ye want in the way of food?' asked the girl.

'Well,' said the man, 'I think we could both start with some Irish smoked salmon with your famous soda bread, then I think a sirloin steak for me, medium-rare please, mushrooms and chips. Why not, eh? I'm ravenous, and might as well be hung for a sheep as a lamb, what? And for you, my dear,' he said to his wife, 'what about some freshly caught Lough Corrib salmon with some new potatoes? And a bottle of, yes, I think Burgundy.' The girl appeared nonplussed as she left for the kitchen.

The visitors waited patiently in anticipation. The minutes had stretched into a hungry half hour before the girl returned. With a smile, she said, 'Himself says that if we had that kind of food here, we'd be eatin' it ourselves . . .'

The Fat of the Land

As the last of the customers dawdled, Tom spotted the local butcher, a rotund man who clearly enjoyed his food, tucking into the last scraps of the buffet whilst nodding and smiling jovially to his companion. It put him in mind of a boy from his home town who'd also been known for his jolly frame.

The boy's mother always claimed that he was 'big-boned' when he was younger and the other kids were poking fun at him because of his size. 'Fatso' was the kindest of the names he was called, but he learned to live with it, and only occasionally resorted to the noble art of fisticuffs and using his weight if someone went too far.

He rode with the blows, turned the other cheek, and grew up with his size. Then, just as he was comfortable, they began calling him 'obese'. Not just him, but everybody similarly upholstered. 'Fat' was one thing, 'obese' something completely different. The one was joked about, but with affection, equated with a jolly disposition, as Falstaff in Shakespeare, the Ghost of Christmas Present in Dickens. Cheery, rubicund maidens and shepherdesses abounded merrily on the canvases of Rubens. Les Dawson was fat. Fat meant fun. The other was stigma. Literally an insupportable weight on the nation's healthcare professionals, the obese man or woman was more to be pitied than laughed at. And it was self-inflicted, an irresponsible mark of weak self-control.

He hadn't put on any weight lately, his belt buckle was in the same notch, but he felt fatter, with all that stuff in the media, and for the first time in his life, he began to feel self-conscious about his weight. It was getting him down. Then some eejit went on record as saying that obesity was a greater danger to public well-being than climate change. Which only com-pounded his anxiety, since some other gobdaw in public office had said earlier that climate change was a bigger threat to the world than terrorism. Now he wasn't just damaging the nation's health, but putting the entire world at risk by his very existence.

He used to be such an easy guy; his leaner, fitter, six-packed friends envied his success with women. He liked them slim and leggy, and they seemed to flock to his side. They all said that he gave them something solid to hold on to, as he laughed them into bed. Now, he felt his self-confidence slipping away, as the 'obese' tag gnawed away at him. In his anxiety, he found himself eating more of the usual bad stuff that piled on the pounds. How could anybody possibly love a big lump of blubber like himself?

Over the years he'd tried the miracle diets that guaranteed the weight would fall off him just by eating only protein, or cabbage, or nothing at all for two days a week. They gave him bad breath, wind that would have frightened a gorilla in the mist, headaches and a sense of humour bypass. The gym was another pointless exercise in every sense; he took one look at the weights, the machines, the sweaty bodies, and knew that he would never expose himself to such indignity. And the same went for squeezing himself into Lycra, which he knew he'd never be able to get out of . . .

He'd given the Saturday tennis-club hop a miss for a couple of weeks, telling the boys in the pub that he had a lot of studying to catch up on, if he wasn't going to get turfed out of the College of Surgeons, where he was supposed to be training to be a doctor. But Jason, his best friend, knew him well enough to suspect that there was another reason for his lack of enthusiasm for chatting up the birds. 'Forget it,' he said, 'you're coming to the feckin' hop; I'm sick of standin' on me own during the ladies' choice.'

He realized how much he'd been missing it as soon as they got there; the music, the laughter, the heady air of anticipation. He knew most of the fellas and girls there, and lots of them smiled and waved at him, glad to see old Fatso back in the land of the living. He saw her the minute he walked through the door, a face he hadn't seen before, and, true to the principle of pulling the birds that he had long explained to those less fortunate in the art: 'Always go for the best-looking girl in the room, she'll be the loneliest, because most of the fellas think they won't have a chance with her, and that she'd turn them down.' So, forgetting his recent lack of confidence, and carried away by the old rush of blood to the head, he made a bee-line for the new face.

They got on like a house on fire, but then, he'd always known how to talk to women. He'd never lost it, his pal Jason thought, as he watched the maestro at work. They danced and chatted, he bought her a Coke, and asked if he could see her home. Sorry, she said, she lived on the other side of town, and had come in a friend's car. Could he see her again? She'd love that, she said, and gave him her phone number. The hop finished with the usual slow waltz, they held each other close, he walked her to her friend's car, she brushed his cheek with a kiss, and she was gone. 'The great Fatso fails to pull!' scoffed his friend, and he just smiled.

He didn't have a car, so he took the bus to see her. She lived with three other girls in a rented house on the Southside. He got on well with her flatmates, country girls like herself, all at university. She welcomed him with a little kiss. She was warm, funny and flirtatious, and he hadn't had a better time without a drink or sex, ever. The last bus was long gone to the terminus when he said goodbye, on his way with a longer, more lingering kiss on her doorstep. Medical students can't afford taxis, and it took him nearly an hour and a half to walk home to the Northside. It was the most exercise he'd taken in his life.

It became a regular trek, across the city by bus, home by what his Da called 'Shank's mare'. Never more than a chat, a laugh and a couple of kisses, and always hanging on in hope until the last bus had gone. Three times a week he would march across the empty city, and fall into bed, knackered, but happy.

Jason persuaded him to join the lads for what used to be the regular get-together in their local, and he had to fend off their comments about his disappearance for weeks. Had he been ill? They said he was certainly not looking his usual self, and if he lost any more weight, he'd have to avoid going out in a high wind. He told them to drink up, give it a rest; he'd had enough of that lately from his Ma.

Jason said it could only be the one thing — love. Fatso laughed it off. He took the bus as usual on Monday, and she welcomed him with a smile, as he joined her and the other girls in their warm front room. There were always other young men there, passing boyfriends that seemed to change with the weather, but this evening there was just one, older, better dressed than the scruffy young fellas like himself. They shook hands as she introduced the new man as Daniel. He'd sensed her suppressed excitement the moment she welcomed him, and she could no longer hold it in. Flushed and laughing with the kind of pleasure he'd never seen in her before, she almost screamed, 'Everybody! Great news! Daniel has asked me to marry him, and I've said yes!'

The other girls joined in the screaming, admiring her new ring, with congratulations, tears and cries of

'About time, Daniel! Two years! We thought you'd never pop the question!' Daniel smiled modestly, and went to get the champagne that he'd brought with him to celebrate the great occasion. Fatso joined in the cheers and the champagne, shaking the happy couple's hands warmly. When he'd finished his drink, he took her gently aside. 'Can I use your phone?' he asked. 'And do you think Daniel would loan me a couple of quid? I'm going to call a taxi.'

The End of the Party

He'd always liked female customers, the open flirta-
tion with the young, single ones, the more guarded,
but no less flirtatious words and smiles with the
young married women. But that's all it ever was.
Even when Tom was young and single himself,
and – as a teller in a country branch – regarded as
something of a catch by the daughters of rural shop-
keepers and farmers, and particularly their mothers,
he never took his chances with the girls. Too risky
– he didn't want to get stuck with a wife and kids in
the back of beyond. Now, he wished he'd let himself
go a bit more. He'd met Maureen when they were
both teenagers at a bank social, an on-and-off casual
relationship for several years, but all their friends,
and their parents, knew it would only end one way,
with Maureen's father leading her up the aisle. As a
bank employee herself, she'd understood, and been
true, constant and uncomplaining about the shifting
all over the country in his pursuit of the Holy Grail

of bank manager, which was at last his. The children hadn't liked being uprooted from friends every few years, but boarding school solved the problem in teenage years, the eldest was now at university, and Tom hoped her brother would follow her. If not, there was always the bank.

At last, the final guest had been decanted through the door, and his staff had slipped away around the corner to the pub for a restorative pint. They'd invited Tom to join them, and he was sorely tempted, but he felt he'd only put a managerial damper on their probably raucous revisiting of the day. Captain of the ship, just himself left, apart from the porter, making a desultory effort to clear up the debris of dirty glasses and half-eaten food.

'Leave it, Dawson,' he said, 'the catering company will clear it up in the morning. I'm on my way, just lock up after I've gone, and thanks for all your hard work.'

Outside, the street and shop window lights were on, brightening the dusk. Tom made his way to his car, unsure of how to end the day. He got in, and sat behind the wheel, remembering his first-ever car, bought for him for two hundred quid by his Da. A second-hand banger, black, with a dodgy passenger

seat. How many miles had he travelled in the faith-
ful old jalopy, up and down the country to rugby
matches, and bank offices, parties, pubs, hops and
even dinner dances, all on a wing and a prayer, on
remoulded tyres and leaking oil? And here he was,
twenty-five years on, still sitting in a second-hand car.
A better one, of course, he'd been through a few
since they took the old Morris to the knacker's yard,
but still second-hand. This was it then, he reflected,
the end of the rainbow, without the pot of gold.
No more rungs of the ladder left to climb. The
engine groaned into life, and he turned her towards
town. He wanted to be alone with his thoughts, with
a pint of stout and a plate of egg and chips, in the
Bankers' Club.

extracts reading groups
competitions books new events extracts
discounts extracts extracts discounts events
competitions reading groups
books new books extracts events reading groups
events new discounts
extracts new books reading groups reading groups
interviews new
events extracts extracts events books
discounts new
new books events events interviews
events new new books
discounts extracts discounts books
www.panmacmillan.com
extracts events reading groups
competitions books extracts new